Zamboni Brez

Zamboni Brez

Mark Fidler

BLR Books
Belmont, Massachusetts

Zamboni Brez

Cover art by K.E. Roehr

BLR Books
#163
464 Common Street
Belmont, MA 02478

ISBN: 0-9721839-1-4

To the caring and committed youth hockey coaches everywhere.

Special thanks to Marty, Jon, Tom, Barry, Dave, Joe, Bob, Ray, and all the assistants and in-house coaches who taught the game of hockey to my own boys.

This book is especially dedicated to Kevin Keefe.

Chapter 1

This is a story about my father. His name is Nikolay Breznikov. Nikolay is a Russian name, and it's pronounced Nee-kol-eye. Almost no one here knows that his first name is Nikolay. Come to think of it, almost no one here knows that his last name is Breznikov. People in America were mostly afraid to pronounce his name, and so he shortened it to Brez, and people just called him 'the Zamboni guy,' or 'Zamboni Brez.' Even today, when I'm out with my father, we run into people who light up when they see him, and say, "Zamboni Brez, how ya doin!"

I can't really tell you about my father without talking about the rest of my family, because our stories are all pretty connected. If it weren't for Yuriy, Katya and me, and our youth hockey, my father might still just be known as 'the Zamboni guy.' I'll start the story two years ago, back when I was a Pee Wee.

For those of you who only know about youth hockey in Russia or in Canada, a Pee Wee in the United States is a hockey player who is twelve or thirteen years old. It's the level after a Squirt and before a Bantam. I was thirteen that season, which means that I was a second year Pee Wee. My name is Stas, but that didn't mean as much to me as being a second year Pee Wee, and being a Shark.

"*How was practice?*" my father asked in Russian as I stepped into the door of our apartment.

"English!" my mother said as she followed me into the front hall.

My father just grunted and walked away. He didn't even wait to hear me tell about my first practice with the Sharks. He always did that when my mother made him speak in English, which meant that he pretty much never completed a conversation, never mind a sentence.

Even speaking in Russian, my father never had too much to say. "A man is what a man does," he used to say. In America, they say that actions speak louder than words. That's what my father believed. If the words had to be in English, actions did all his speaking. I wondered why he even came to this country if he didn't want to try to learn the language. Actually, I think that he understood English enough, but he just refused to speak it.

My English wasn't perfect back then, but it was okay. We had moved to America three years earlier, when I was ten. We used to live in Moscow. I still had a heavy Russian accent, but I could say whatever I needed to say in English, and people understood. I was pretty proud of the way I could talk after just three years in this country. My brother Yuriy could speak better than I could, and he was only eleven, but he didn't have as many years of Russian to undo. We also had learned English in school when we were in Russia, something my father never did. My sister Katya was seven, and sounded as American as any kid I knew. Sometimes I was jealous of the way she spoke. Other times, I was proud of my accent.

My father had worked the early shift that day at the rink, so I wanted to tell him all about the Shark's practice, but the conversation was clearly over. Instead, I lugged my hockey bag back to my bedroom, where I stacked it on top of my brother's bag at the foot of our bunk beds. It was just as well I hadn't talked with my father. He would have criticized everything I told him. He used to play on the Red Army hockey club in Moscow, and American hockey was never good enough for him.

"How was practice?" my brother Yuriy asked in his high pitched voice which contained just a hint of a Russian accent.

"Great," I said without enthusiasm.

"How were the kids? Were they any good?"

"Yeah, they seemed really good," I said, getting a little more excited. "There were some huge kids. We even have a girl on the team, and she's pretty big. I wasn't even the biggest guy on the team!"

"That's unbelievable," Yuriy said, and it was. I had always been the biggest kid on every hockey team I had played on. But this was the Eastern Massachusetts Select Hockey League. Everyone just called it E Mass. All the best kids from Boston to Hartford played in this league. And the top teams in the league got to play for the Montreal Cup, which was the best youth hockey tournament in the world. Everyone said that the E Mass teams won it a lot. E Mass coaches liked size, and if two kids trying out for a team were about the same in skill, they always picked the bigger guy. I had heard that the Shark coach especially liked big guys, which is one reason I tried out for that team. They also practiced at the rink my father worked at, in Hingham, which made it easy for me to get there.

"You're lucky," Yuriy continued. "My team's gonna stink this year. It's not fair that you can play E Mass hockey and I have to play town hockey."

"You never know. Maybe all those kids moving up from Mites are really good."

"But they're tiny!" Yuriy said. "You should have seen them in the tryouts!"

"So what? You're just a Squirt, and Squirts can't check in your league, so being little doesn't matter that much."

"I still wish I was playing in your league."

"Don't worry," I said. "Mama and Papa said that you can play E Mass when you're thirteen. That is, if you're good enough."

"Good enough?" Yuriy bellowed. "I'm much better than you were when you were eleven! That's why they should let me play E Mass this year."

"It's a ton of money. They can't afford it."

"I could deliver papers like you do."

"I only do that in the summer, when Kenny, the regular paperboy, is on vacation. I fill in for him. And that only pays for part of the cost," I said. "We barely have enough to pay for the rest."

"So, how will they have enough money in two years?"

"I don't know. They said you could play then, so they'll figure out a way to pay."

"So these kids on your team, Stas, are they good, or just big?"

"Both," I said, and grinned. Yuriy grinned back. While size did not mean as much in his league, it made all the difference in the world in Pee Wees. Yuriy was a big fan of college and pro hockey, and understood the importance of size. A lot of coaches would rather have a big guy who's slow than a little guy who's fast.

"Are they nice?" Yuriy asked.

"I guess," I said, though I didn't really think so. Not a single kid had said a word to me the whole practice. Of course, I never said a single word to any of them, either. But I was the new guy. It's a lot harder to be the new guy. I didn't even know the names of all the other kids yet.

"What about your coach?" Yuriy asked.

My coach. Oh, god, I thought. All the guy did was yell. I just hoped that he knew more hockey than my town coaches the past two years. Even though I was glad to live in America, my coaches in Russia had been much better. The main reason my parents had let me play in the E Mass league was so that I would get better coaching. I just hoped that Coach Murphy was like my fourth grade teacher two years before. Mr. Kavikola had seemed really scary the first month of school, but by the end of the year, I loved him. He was pretty strict, but he was also a great teacher. Maybe I'd feel that same way about Coach Murphy by the end of the season.

"I think he'll be good," I said. "He wants to win. He's going to take us to the Montreal Cup."

"What's that?" Yuriy asked.

"You don't know what the Montreal Cup is?" I asked, rolling my eyes in disgust.

Yuriy shook his head no.

"It's only the top youth hockey tournament in the whole world. Teams from every serious hockey country come and play for a week. They're all Triple-A select teams, and the winner is the world champion."

"Wow!" Yuriy said.

Yeah, wow, I thought, still not quite believing that I was on an E Mass team with a shot at playing for the Montreal Cup.

Chapter 2

"Stas, tell your father about your new team," my mother said as she filled my bowl with *borshch*.

"They're called the Sharks, Mama."

How could she not remember that? She always called it my new team. Everyone knows about the Sharks. Papa's been making their ice ever since he started working at the Ice Forum!

My mother leaned over me to pour the soup into Katya's bowl.

"No!" my little sister shrieked.

"Katya, what is it?" my mother asked with a trace of alarm in her voice.

"I hate *borshch*!"

"You are hungry enough, you will like it," my father said.

"I don't want it! I don't like the beets."

"Tatiana, pour it!" my father said. "What kind of Russian does not eat *borshch*? She will eat it."

My mother hesitated, then filled Katya's bowl with the bright red cabbage and beet soup. When my father spoke like that, people obeyed him, even my mother.

"What was I saying before?" my mother asked.

"You wanted Stas to tell Papa about his new team," Yuriy said.

"Oh, yes. So, tell your father about the kids, and the coaches. They have a new head coach. Your father does not know of him."

I looked across the table at my father. He continued to eat, as if ignoring my mother, but I saw him secretly eyeing me. I knew that he wanted to hear about my hockey team, even if he did not ask.

6

"One kid, Peter Donohue, his father used to play on the Kings. But Peter is the alternate, which means he only plays if one of our regular guys is hurt. Peter knows tons about hockey, though. He's like a walking CD of hockey facts. Our goalie is Mac, and he's unbelievable. And this kid, Eddie, he's huge and he loves to hit. And all the kids are really good, Papa. None of the kids on my town "A" team last year would have had a chance of playing on this team, except maybe Jimmy Duval. And that's just because Jimmy is a goon, and I think this coach likes goons."

"You're big, but you're no galavarez," Papa said to me in Russian. A *galavarez* is a thug. It actually means 'head chopper' in Russian.

"What did he say?" Katya asked. Katya was my seven year-old sister.

"Nikolay, look! Your own daughter cannot understand you when you speak in Russian. You must learn your new language."

"O bozhe!"

"Nikolay! Do not curse!"

"It's very sad," he went on to say in Russian. *"My own little girl, and she can't understand her papa. She hates borshch. The only thing Russian about her is her name."*

"Mama," Katya whined, pinching her nose between sips of the soup, "tell me what he's saying!"

"If he cares for you to know," my mother said coldly, "he will speak it in English."

She stared across the table at my father who stopped chewing and stared right back at her. His huge hand tightened around his spoon, but he said nothing. My mother held his stare for a few seconds longer, then she looked down and continued to eat. My brother and I stopped eating, and exchanged fearful glances. I peeked at my father, and he finally moved his eyes away from my mother and looked at my sister. As soon as his eyes touched upon Katya, his whole face softened and a sad smile crept to his lips.

"I am sorry, Katya," my father said slowly, in English. "I will try more hard to speak in the English. It be not easy for me, but I know it be important to do."

"So what were you saying, Papa?" Katya asked.

"I do not remember. Something is about hockey."

"You said that Stas was not a goon," Yuriy said. "You'd never know that if you saw him play street hockey with me in the yard. He nailed me yesterday, and I have this huge bruise, right on the butt. Let me show you."

Yuriy stood up and began to unbutton his pants.

"Yuriy," my mother said, "there is no need to show us."

"I want to see it!" Katya said.

"Katya!" my mother said, throwing her a stern look.

"*No respectable girl wants to see –,*" my father began in Russian.

"Achh!" my mother cried.

My father continued, in English. "My wife scream every time I speak in my native tongue, my son is *galavarez* and my daughter is tramp. America is great country." He shook his head in disgust.

"Nikolay," my mother said. "*Tikho*! Be quiet! You speak foolishness!"

"At least he's speaking it in English," Yuriy said.

"Aargh!" Papa cried, as he put down his spoon and got up from the table.

"Yuriy, apologize to your father! Nikolay, please do not leave the table. We must eat together! We are family!"

"Papa," Yuriy began.

My father was out of the room, and the silence at the table was deafening. Finally, my mother spoke.

"I try to keep our family together, and see what happens? I spend forever driving you boys to hockey and waiting in cold rinks. Stas, in the summer I drive every morning to get your papers. I spend money on hockey skates and sticks when I can barely afford to buy groceries. I do all this for family, and no one is happy. What can I do?"

Tears welled up in my mother's eyes, and my heart grew heavy.

"It's okay, Mama," I said. "American families fight at the dinner table. It's normal in this country."

"How do you know it's normal? You are from Russia."

"TV! American families are always arguing at the dinner table on TV shows. You should watch *Malcolm in the Middle.* So don't feel bad."

My mother smiled at me and said, "Thank you for saying that, but Russian families do not act that way. Russian children respect their parents. My hope is that in some ways you will be American and in some ways you will be Russian."

Chapter 3

I eyed the guy next to me as Coach Murphy put the whistle to his mouth. I thought the kid's name was Billy, but I wasn't sure. The coach's head moved forward, and the whistle shrieked, and then he tossed a puck into the corner.

I moved my legs as fast as I could, but my large frame could only go so quickly. The other guy, who did turn out to be called Billy, was one of the few small guys on the team, and his short legs were lightning quick. Halfway to the corner, he was a step ahead of me. *O bozhe*, I wanted to get to that puck first!

Instinct kicked in, and I slowed up a hair, giving me just enough time to see which way he would turn with the puck. I saw him cut to the inside, and then I accelerated. Just as Billy had the puck on his stick, I lowered my shoulder and slammed into him.

Boom! His shoulder pads and helmet crashed into the boards, making a sound that echoed throughout the curved-ceiling rink. Billy went down and I picked up the loose puck and took it toward the goal. Mac was out of position, and I fired the puck into the half-empty net.

Score! I raised my stick, and then noticed that Mac was skating away from me, heading toward the corner. Billy lay crumpled on the ice, not moving. A wave of guilt shot through me. I hadn't meant to hurt him. I was just doing what I was supposed to do. I followed Mac over to see how Billy was. As I edged my way in, Mac turned around and pushed me away.

"Get out of here!" Mac said, poking me in the ribs with the fat knob at the butt end of his goalie stick. "Give him some space! What's wrong with you anyway? This is a practice! Billy is your teammate!"

A number of the other boys skated past me toward Billy. Most ignored me. Some gave me dirty looks. As I was standing alone near the face-off circle, feeling like a total dork, one of the boys skated up to me.

"Don't feel bad. The kid slipped as he pivoted, otherwise he wouldn't be hurt. It's not your fault."

"That's not what they think," I said, pointing the butt end of my stick toward my teammates, who were still surrounding Billy.

"Billy's their friend. They'll get over it. You'll be their friend, too, soon."

"Thanks. By the way, my name's Stas," I said to the boy.

"Stas?"

"Yeah, is there something wrong with that name?" I said defensively.

"Uh, no," the boy said. "It's just that I never heard of that name. I'm Ben. I'm a new kid, too. I know two of the other guys from my school team. Sully and Bake. They're pretty nice, and you'll like them, too, when you get to know them. Some of the kids are mad because their friends got cut so we could make this team. They'll be fine when they get to know us, especially if we help this team win more games, and I think we will."

I smiled at Ben. "I hope so."

As I spoke, my eyes moved back to Billy. He moved his left leg. Phew! I had been afraid he was dead. My mother always sighed in relief when a kid who went down finally moved. She always worried that he might be paralyzed like Travis Roy, a guy who played for BU and got paralyzed in his first college game. My mom says that if you move, then whatever's broken will eventually heal. Billy moved, and so I knew he'd be okay. I prayed that he was not seriously hurt. I never wanted to really hurt anyone, especially a teammate, and especially on the second day of practice with a new team. If Billy missed a couple months of the season with a broken bone, all of the other kids would hate me.

Slowly, Billy pushed himself up to a sitting position. My teammates all tapped their sticks on the ice as Coach Murphy helped him to his feet. I touched my stick to the ice a couple of times as well. Billy skated slowly toward the bench while Coach Murphy skated toward me.

Uh oh, I thought. I'm in real trouble now.

"Stas," my coach said, "I like your attitude."

I smiled nervously.

"A lot of very talented players did not make this team, as you know. Now you, you have your share of talent, but you have something else that those other boys do not have. You know what that is?"

I wasn't sure what to say, and so I said nothing.

"Stas, you have size, and you know how to use it. I know that you weren't born with a silver spoon in your mouth, and you play that way. I like it. Got it?"

My short, muscular coach winked at me.

"Just take it a bit easier on our own boys. You hit like that every practice, we won't have a team to compete with. Let's save most of that for the other team. Okay?"

I nodded.

"Now, get in line for the next drill!"

He patted me hard on my shoulder pad, and I skated off. As I approached the other players, I didn't know how I felt. I was relieved that Coach Murphy hadn't yelled at me. In fact, he liked what I had done to Billy! The problem was, I didn't really like it. I felt bad about hurting him. Was my coach going to want me to hurt kids on the other team in games? And then he had talked about talent. Was he saying that I didn't have as much talent as the other kids? I had lots of talent, but never had a coach to really bring it out in me. My father always said that I was loaded with ability, but I was still a little rough around the edges. An unfinished product, he called me.

That's why he signed me up for E Mass hockey. It was the best there was. The best players. The best coaches. My father wanted me to play for the Sharks because the old coach used to coach a college team, and his teams always played a well disciplined game. But that coach got transferred to Toronto in his regular job, and so the Sharks had this new coach. My father didn't know Coach Murphy. His uncle used to play in the NHL, for the Red Wings, and the team hired him, and so my father and I figured that he'd be great. So far, though, I wasn't too impressed. The first few practices on any team are mostly just boring skating drills, and so I wasn't too worried. He'd be good, I was sure.

I stood in line for the next drill, full ice figure-eights, forwards and then backwards. I felt the guy behind me pushing at me, and I moved forward, bumping the kid in front of me.

"Hey, cut it out!" the boy said.

"Sorry," I said.

"Yeah, sure you are."

I *was* sorry. I didn't want to cause any trouble, but none of the kids would talk with me, except that new kid, Ben.

"Sully, move up," a big kid two places ahead in line said. "I'll move back there. He can push me all he wants."

Sully and the big kid switched places in line. Was this guy going to fight me? I was almost afraid to stay in my spot in line, but I was more afraid to move. He'd think I was a wimp, and that's the last thing you want to be in hockey. I'd rather have kids hate me than think I'm a wimp.

Waiting in line, the big guy turned his head, and spoke over his shoulder, "You're the Ruskie, right?"

"Huh?"

"The Ruskie. The Russian kid. You're from Russia, right?"

"I used to live in Russia. But I'm American now. My mother is going to be a citizen soon, and then I'll be a full American, too."

"I'm Eddie. Eddie Germano. Don't be embarrassed about being Russian. I love the Ruskies. They're the nastiest hockey players. They've won a ton of Olympic gold medals. They would have beaten team Canada back in the 70's except Bobby Clarke broke the ankle of their star player. I saw it at the Hockey Hall of Fame."

"My name's Stas. You've been to the Hockey Hall of Fame?"

"Twice."

"Where is it?" I asked.

"Toronto."

"Toronto! That's in Canada! That's where the old Shark coach moved!"

"O'Neil, right. Coach O'Neil played wuss hockey. My father would have yanked me from the team if O'Neil had stayed. But this guy Murphy is supposed to be one tough dude. Murphy never made the NHL. My father had heard about him from Juniors. I guess he ended a few careers there."

I didn't want to ask Eddie what he meant by that. Did he hit people so hard that they never recovered? Did he ever paralyze anyone? Did he kill anyone? I shuddered.

"Well, Stas, I'm on this team, you're on this team, and that's Murphy's kid over there."

Eddie pointed to a short kid in a red practice jersey.

"Little Murph is not that big, but he makes up for it with his checking. I saw him play for Southie Pee Wees last year, and the boy can hit. It was his first year ever playing check hockey, but man, could he hit. Because he's not so tall, the refs let his elbows come up higher. They say that he sharpens his elbows each time he gets his skates sharpened."

I looked nervously into Eddie's eyes, and saw him laugh. He was just kidding. Of course he was. No one would actually sharpen their elbows.

And then the whistle blew, and Eddie took off down the ice. He moved pretty well for a big guy. Seconds later, the whistle blew again and it was my turn. I worked as hard as I could, even if it was a boring drill.

Chapter 4

"Man, you reek," Ben said to me as I was pulling off my black jersey.

"You don't exactly smell like roses yourself," I said.

"Thank God," Ben said. "If my mother had her way, she'd wash all my stuff after every practice."

"My mother makes me wash everything at the end of the season."

"Just once a year?" Ben asked as he stepped out of his hockey pants.

"People don't wash clothes as much in Russia. Yuriy wears a shirt once and puts it in the hamper, and my mother has a fit. When she first came to this country, she couldn't believe that most Americans washed their clothes after each time they wore them."

"Who's Yuriy?"

"My brother," I said, as I tossed my cup into my hockey bag.

"Stas, don't do that," Eddie said from the bench across from me.

"Do what?"

"Toss your cup through the air. If that gets washed just once a year, it must collect a pretty nasty bunch of germs. Makes me want to hold my breath."

"So, what should I do? Should I wear my cup home?" I asked.

"No, stupid. Just place it in slowly. Cuts down on the waft factor. In another month you won't even have to throw it. It'll be so ripe it'll be able to walk to the bag itself. It can just follow its nose."

I smiled, then looked toward Lizzy, the one girl on our team. Suddenly, I felt embarrassed. Should we be talking about cups and stuff in front of her? Our eyes met, and she must have read my thoughts, because she said, "Don't shut up because of me. I have four brothers. You can't say anything I haven't heard before, and there's nothing I haven't seen, either."

"Don't be so sure," Eddie said, grinning.

"Eddie, you're a loser," one of the other kids said, tossing a tape ball at him.

Eddie ignored the kid, and continued to take off his equipment. The guys all got undressed down to their boxers. Obviously, with Lizzy there, that's as far as anyone went. But I don't think it would have been different even if Lizzy weren't there. No one ever got naked the year before when I played Pee Wees for Braintree. Next year, it would be different. Lots of Bantams are in high school, and they say that everyone actually takes a shower after practice there. And at Braintree High, there's just one giant shower with all the guys in it at the same time. At least that was what I'd heard. That sounded pretty gross to me. And what they say about towel snapping sounded even worse. I was in no hurry to go to high school

"Hey, Stas," Ben said quietly to me, "where do you live?"

"Braintree."

"Any chance you can drop me off in Quincy on the way home? I live right off the highway. Otherwise, I have to wait an hour for my mother to get out of work."

"Sure, I'll ask my father. Hey, wait a sec. I'm not leaving for a while. My father's working here for another hour. He's driving me home because my mother is with Yuriy."

"That's okay. We can hang out together while we wait."

"Sure," I said.

"So, your father works here?" Ben asked. "At the rink?"

"Yeah, he drives the Zamboni."

"Your father drives the Zamboni?" the kid on my other side asked.

"Uh huh."

"Brez? Is your last name Brez?"

"Breznikov. It's Breznikov."

"Your father is Zamboni Brez!" another boy said.

"Is that what they call him?" I asked.

"Yeah. He's the best. The ice used to bite at this rink until he came here two years ago."

"How long have you been playing here?" I asked, stepping into my slippery black sports pants.

"I played Hingham Youth Hockey here before the Sharks. I started when I was three. My parents tell me I was skating before I was walking, so I know this ice."

"What's your name?"

"Dan. Dan McPhee. But everyone calls me Moose."

I could see why. He was huge and hairy! He looked like he even shaved!

"I'm Stas."

"I know."

Just then, Eddie Germano walked across the skate room mat. He strutted bare chested, while below his waist he was still wearing all his equipment. Eddie's bulging pecs and beefy upper arms were huge! I quickly put my own shirt on, covering up my less developed upper body.

"Hey, Eddie, watch it!" one boy yelled. "You almost cut my freaking toes off."

"Chill," Eddie said. "I'm good with these skates. I haven't removed any body parts with these blades yet, at least not any toes." Eddie flashed a big grin at me.

"Hey Stas, move that big butt of yours over a bit. I need to sit down here. That's my bag there under the bench."

I moved over and Eddie sat between Ben and me.

"Oh man, I'm tired," Eddie said loudly. "That coach, he's crazy! I never had a coach make us do suicides up to nine before. At least not the second day of practice!"

"Looks like you enjoyed your off season a bit too much," one of the other kids said to Eddie, patting his own stomach.

"Drew, are you trying to tell me that this is fat?" Eddie said, jiggling his own bare stomach.

"Either that, or you bought a little extra protective padding."

"Hey," Eddie said, flexing his muscles, "this here is rock solid. This is a body by Boyd. You're talking to next year's poster child for Rick Boyd's Fitness and Training."

"Yeah, Eddie," another boy called out, "you're the 'before' picture."

All the boys on the team laughed. I glanced at Eddie, who was smiling.

"Just jealous, boys, especially Drew, our resident ninety-nine pound weakling. Some of us are *men*," Eddie said, then paused, and continued in a very high, almost girlish voice, "and some of you are still *boys*."

"If you're a man," Mac, our goalie, said, "then I'm in no hurry to grow up."

"You don't hurry to do much, especially in the net. My mother always hated to come to my games because she couldn't see the play without slow motion, that is until you joined the team last year."

"That's all right, Eddie. I don't need to be quick. With you on defense, all you need to do is to stand near the net and there's no room for the puck to possibly get in. I can just nap."

"Nothing new about that, Mac."

The kids on the team were all smiling as they packed their bags full of wet, smelly clothing and equipment. Just then, Coaches Murphy and Regan walked into the team skate room.

"Good practice, boys," Coach Regan said. "It was awful hot out there, and there were a lot of summer fries and milk shakes that needed working off."

"Eddie!" one of the kids whispered loudly.

"Hey," Coach Murphy said, "for his size, Eddie skates as fast as anyone out there. I already feel bad for the other guys this year. He'll be like a freight train heading for them in the corners."

Eddie stood up, bare-chested and still wearing his hockey pants. He flexed his muscles and took a bow. The other boys all smiled.

"I can see it's going to be a fun season this year," Coach Murphy said. "You guys have unbelievable talent. If our physical game is half as good, no one'll touch us. Montreal, here we come."

"And guys," Coach Regan added, "remember we have three new players with us this year. We had a good season last year because we really pulled together as a team. Make sure you guys all get to know Ben, Stas and James over there, James Murphy. Bring them into the fold."

I looked around at the other kids on the team. A few glanced at me and nodded. Most just sat there. A couple, including Mac, flashed me dirty looks.

"Next practice, Thursday, at six," Coach Regan said. "Let me know if any of you need a practice schedule."

The two coaches left.

"Hey Billy," Mac said sarcastically, "let's welcome these new players to the team, especially the Commie." He looked at me.

"Come on, Mac," Woody said. "Forget about it. Billy's all right."

"Yeah," another kid said, "Billy goes down once a day anyway. He either likes to scare his mom, or he finds the ice comfortable, like a mattress."

"Myself, I like a nice warm waterbed," a different kid said. "But everyone likes their own thing. Uncle Fester used to sleep on a bed of nails. Billy likes hard ice. Billy, you didn't really get hurt, right?"

"Right, Will," Billy said. "I'm fine."

"No thanks to the little Red over there," Mac said, looking right at me.

"Mac, lay off him," Sully said. "Nobody got hurt. Stas is on our team, and I don't know about you, but when these games get nasty this season, like they always do, I'll be glad to have Stas on my side."

"What about me?" Eddie asked, with a trace of a hurt expression on his face.

"Eddie," Drew said, "you know that we're glad to have you."

"Yeah," another boy said, "you protect us on the ice, and make us all feel smarter when we're talking off the ice."

"How do I do that?" Eddie asked.

"Figure it out. I'll give you a hint. You're doing it now."

The whole team laughed.

"What do you mean?" Eddie asked.

Everyone laughed even harder. Even I laughed.

Chapter 5

"Did you see any of our practice, Papa?" I asked my father as he was starting the car.

"*A little,*" he answered in Russian.

"Shouldn't you be practicing your English?"

The car lurched out of the parking lot and merged between two fast moving cars on the main road.

"*You sound like your mother,*" he answered in Russian.

"Don't you think that it would be easier if you could talk English better, like Mama says?"

"*What about you? How would you remember your mother tongue if you did not hear it from me? I understand English. I just make ice and sweep floors, and so understanding is enough.*"

I shrugged and said nothing. We drove for a while in silence.

"*Do you like your new coach?*" my father asked me, still speaking in Russian.

"I don't know."

"*You do have some very strong players on that team.*"

"It's an E Mass team. All the E Mass teams are really strong. It's a tough league. The kids say it's the best in all New England. Do you think it really is?"

"*I only know the teams that play here, which are the town teams and the E Mass teams. I would not know about any other leagues. I do know that the Shark teams last year were quite strong, and your team was very well coached.*"

"Coach Murphy likes hitting."

"Humph."

"Hitting is an important part of the game. You told me that last year when I moved up to Pee Wees."

"It is a part of the game, but at your age, the ice is still large, and skating and puck control will beat size. Those skills are also more difficult to develop, and that is what boys your age need to be working on. In four years, the ice will be smaller. With bigger and faster skaters, you need to hit in order to win."

"Well, we have this kid Eddie Germano. He's so big and tough, he's scary. I think he'll help us win."

My father said nothing. We finished the ride home in silence. I wanted to turn on the radio, but my father hated the stations that I liked, and I wasn't exactly wild about what he listened to. It sounded like dentist office music.

As we rounded the corner onto our street, I saw Yuriy in Greene's driveway, shooting an orange ball at Brendan. Brendan Greene was only seven years old, the same age as Katya, but he had the best driveway for street hockey, and he was always happy to play goalie. He liked to play with any big kids, and to Brendan, Yuriy and I were big kids.

My father pulled the car up to the curb in front of the three family house we lived in. I jumped out the door and raced across the street.

"Hey Stas," Yuriy said.

"Hi, Stas," Brendan said.

"Can I shoot some?" I asked. "Yuriy, can I borrow your stick?"

Yuriy handed me his street hockey stick. It was a little short, but I could still rip 'em with it.

"How was practice?" Yuriy said. "More fun than the first?"

I lined up the hard, plastic orange ball and leaned into a slap shot. It whistled over Brendan's left shoulder and hit the twine in the upper corner.

"Ah, okay."

"Okay?" Yuriy said. "That's all? We're talking about hockey, here. You *love* hockey! And this is Shark hockey!"

"Yeah, but we're still mostly doing get-in-shape skating drills. And the kids, well, you know, I'm the new guy and all. They're not the easiest group of kids to know."

Brendan slid the ball back to me and I lined it up for another shot.

"Jerks, huh?"

I pulled my stick back, and fired a wicked hard slap shot. It went right into Brendan's homemade foam pads. Dang.

"Nice save, Brendan," I said, then turned to Yuriy. "Some kids are jerks. One guy especially. The goalie. He seems to hate me. I think that some of his friends got cut from the team because of me. Plus, I wrecked this kid Billy in practice, and I think that Billy is his friend. He called me a Commie and a Red."

"Why?"

"He's an idiot, that's why."

Brendan kicked the puck back out to me. I shuffled it to my backhand, and lifted one high to the stick side. The puck grazed the crossbar and banged against the garage door just behind the net.

"Almost," Yuriy said.

"Yeah," I said. "His name is Mac, and he doesn't even know that Russia is not a Communist country anymore. I guess he's seen too many movies about the Cold War. I hate it when people think that about Russia. School is bad enough, never mind having to deal with that on my hockey team."

Brendan passed the puck back to me. I quickly flicked a hard shot on the ice. On the driveway, actually. I just *called* it the ice. Brendan's stick was barely off the ice and the puck slid through the five-hole. The five-hole is the crack between the goalie's pads when he splits them into an upside down "V" to cover more of the lower net.

"Maybe this year will be better in school," Yuriy said. "Maybe the middle school will be different."

"I don't think so. You went to Park Elementary with me, but the kids were fine with you. There are just some tough kids in my class."

"You also sound Russian," Yuriy said. "I sound more like an American."

"Yeah," I said. "You're lucky. You were younger when we moved. I really miss Russia. I wish I was still back there. I wouldn't be so different if I lived in Russia."

"Yeah, but our whole family would be living in that tiny two room apartment if we were still in Russia."

"That two room apartment seemed huge back home. Lots of families lived in less. Here, we have twice as much room, but I don't know any other American families that have three kids sharing one bedroom, especially boys and girls together. At least at school, people liked me. And the hockey in Moscow was the best. Any one of those teams would kill any town team that I've played for."

"Yeah," Yuriy said, "but now you're on the Sharks, so your hockey should be as good as it was in Moscow."

I breathed in deeply and slowly exhaled.

"I hope so," I said.

Chapter 6

"Mama, have you heard of Meadows Prep?" I asked between bites of scrambled egg.

"No," she answered as she handed a piece of buttered toast to Katya.

"It's a school. A private school. It's where Ben goes."

"Who is Ben?" my mother asked.

"Ben! You know, one of the other new kids on my hockey team. He goes there, and he said that it's a great school. Maybe I can go there."

"Private school. They charge money to go! Your school is free. End of story."

"But Mama, Meadows Prep is supposed to be the best on the South Shore."

"The best hockey," Yuriy interjected.

"Ah ha!" my mother said, and gave me a knowing smile.

"Yes, the best hockey, but also the best for school work. It's supposed to be really hard. Isn't education one of the main reasons we came to this country?"

"If you do your work in your school now, you will have good education. You do not always do that. Now you want to go to a school which has more work? That does not make sense."

"Except for the hockey," Yuriy said.

"Shut up!" I said.

"How come I can't play hockey?" Katya said.

"You are a girl! Thank goodness your father is at work this morning. If he heard you say this, ay-yi-yi! He worries that America is not good place to grow up a girl. You will do figure skating this winter. We have already paid."

"I hate figure skating!"

"You have never done it. How do you know?"

"You never played hockey either," Yuriy said snidely. "How do you know you'd like that?"

"I play street hockey with you guys and Brendan."

"Yeah, about once a month," Yuriy said.

"Hey, Yuriy," I said, "she can like whatever she wants. Personally, I think she has hockey talent, for a seven year-old and a girl."

"Almost eight," Katya said.

"So, Mama, maybe I can go to Meadows?"

"Maybe money can fall from the heavens, like manna, and then you can go."

"What if I got a scholarship? Ben said that lots of kids go there and get scholarships. Especially hockey players."

"Scholarships?" my mother asked. "That means?"

"That means that you don't have to pay."

"It also means that you have to be smart," Yuriy said. "Forget it."

"Thanks, Yuriy," I said.

"You are everyone's friend this morning, Yuriy," my mother said. "Your brother, he be quite smart. A little lazy, yes, but he has a good brain, just like you do."

"And me, too?" Katya said.

"Of course," my mother said. "Stas, you work hard this year, and get yourself better grades, and yes, if you get scholarship, you can maybe go to that private school. But to get good grades, you must get to school on time, and the bus might be here in two minutes, so eat it up and run!"

I looked at the big round kitchen clock. It was almost seven-thirty! I shoveled in my last two bites of eggs, chugged the last of my orange juice, grabbed my toast for the bus and flew from the table. If I were still in elementary school, I'd have another fifteen minutes until that bus came!

I grabbed my backpack and ran out the front door. Racing up the street, I shoved the last of the toast into my mouth. I spotted about six kids waiting at the corner bus stop. Good. I wasn't late. I stopped running and walked the rest of the way. None of the other kids said a word to me. I didn't really know any of the three girls, and I knew only one of the boys. Jimmy Duval played with me the year before on my town Pee Wee team, but he had barely spoken to me since he found out that I was playing with the Sharks instead of for Braintree.

"Hey, Jimmy," I chirped, trying to sound friendly.

Jimmy nodded back, but didn't crack a smile.

At that moment, the yellow school bus pulled up. I let all the other kids get on before me. They'd been at the bus stop first, and so it only seemed right. Finally, stepping onto the bus, my stomach tightened. I hated this moment, trying to decide where to sit. As usual, the girls were seated in the front of the bus, chewing gum and talking. There were a bunch of free seats in the girl section, but no completely empty ones at the back of the bus. I could have my own seat with the girls, or I could sit next to one of the guys further back. I walked past the girls, and needed to quickly decide who to sit next to. I didn't want to sit next to Jimmy, but I also felt funny sitting beside someone that I didn't know very well. Instinct took over, and I went straight to the hockey player. I think that I was born with a magnet. If it had anything to do with hockey, I was drawn straight to it. I slipped my backpack off my shoulders, and plopped down in the seat next to Jimmy.

Jimmy was staring out the window, and didn't even look at me. Man, was it awkward. Finally, I couldn't stand the silence a second longer.

"So, how's the team look this year?" I asked.

"What's it to you?" he answered.

"You guys are my friends. I've played with you for two years. I want you to do well."

"If you wanted us to do well, you would have stayed with us. We have this little shrimpy guy on the team instead. He'd definitely be on Pee Wee 2 if you were still playing. He's going to get creamed at this level."

"Maybe he has skill, like Brian Gionta. Brian plays in the NHL and has smaller skates than you do."

"And maybe my real name is Wayne Gretzky. Dream on. You could have made a difference, but you'd rather play with a bunch of strangers than with the kids in your own town. No wonder everyone hates you."

"Well, they didn't exactly like me last year, and I wasn't on the Sharks then."

"You were the new guy."

"It was my second year playing with most of those kids!"

"That's still new. Most of the kids on the team were born in Braintree, and most of their parents were South Shore kids growing up. You're from Russia. It takes time to fit in."

"Two years is a pretty long time."

"So, you're saying that you would have stayed with the town if we had been nice to you?" Jimmy said, raising his voice. He was beginning to sound angry, and you don't want to make Jimmy Duval angry.

"I don't know. E Mass hockey is really good. I bet you'd like to play for the Sharks."

"If I was good enough, but I'm not, right?"

I didn't say anything. I wasn't sure what I was going to say. Jimmy wasn't good enough, even for Coach Murphy, who seemed to like goons. Jimmy Duval was slow and had hands of lead. If he got you, though, you probably did not get up.

Luckily, the school bus pulled to a stop. I didn't have to answer Jimmy. I shuffled forward with the crowd and stepped off the bus. Everyone seemed to walk up to some group of kids already in the schoolyard, boys to boys and girls to girls. I watched Jimmy as he joined the hockey gang. Last year, that had been my crowd. I never really felt part of them, but at least I had kids to hang out with. This year would be different. After just one week of school, classes looked like they'd be boring, as usual, but lunch was the worst. Deciding who to sit with was painful.

I was standing awkwardly between two groups of boys, praying that the school bell would ring. I felt that everyone's eyes had to be on me, either laughing at me or feeling sorry for me because I didn't have any friends. I got down on one knee, unzipped my backpack, and began shuffling through my books, as if I were looking for something. Maybe people would think that I needed to find my homework or something before I joined my friends.

Rrrring! At last the bell sounded. Relieved, I zipped up my pack and joined the plodding herd of kids heading for the door.

Chapter 7

"Again!" Coach Murphy shouted. "If you guys can't move faster than that, there's no way we'll ever go to Montreal!"

Montreal. I had only known a little bit about the Montreal Cup before this season. Now I knew teams came from all over the world, from America, Canada, Finland, Germany, Russia. Russia! Oh, to play against the best teams from Russia. I couldn't get it off my mind.

The way it worked was, only the top two teams in the league after the first thirteen games made the tournament. You played each of the other thirteen teams once, and the standings then decided it. After that, the season continued for twenty-six more games, but it did not mean as much. Pee Wee majors in E Mass hockey was all about Montreal, and I wanted to go.

"Stas, get ready!"

I turned my rear skate to the side and prepared to push off with maximum acceleration. The whistle blew, and I was off. I skated as fast as I could to the spot where the blue line met the boards. I was flying! It helped that I was motivated, and one thought kept me going: Montreal. I stopped, crossed over, and sprinted for the far end of the red line. My legs suddenly grew heavy. This was the fourth time that we had done this drill, and each time, that fizz in my legs struck earlier. By the time I hit the red line, I needed to muster every bit of energy I had just to turn my skates and stop. Starting up, my whole body was moving in slow motion.

"Move it, Stas!" Coach Regan yelled.

I was skating as fast as I could, but my legs felt like they were made of lead. There was no juice left. I was out of gas. By the time I did one more zig-zag and stopped at the far goal, I bent over in exhaustion.

The other kids on the team were beat, too. Didn't Coach Murphy know how hard he was working us? I had read in a hockey magazine about muscle recovery time. Didn't my coaches know about that?

"Coach, can we get some water?" Will asked.

"Water?" Coach Murphy bellowed. "You want water? You guys were all so slow, how can you be thirsty? Let's do the corner drill. Maybe that will work up a real thirst in you."

The corner drill! Usually I loved that drill. They moved the net to the corner of the rink, and had it face the glass, leaving about ten feet of ice between the net and the boards. A puck was dropped, and two guys fought it out to get off a shot and score. It usually got very physical, and was incredibly tiring. I didn't know if I had the energy for the corner drill.

Luckily, I was last in line, and so I had a lot of time to rest before it was my turn. I was still thirsty, but my legs no longer felt like rubber. Unluckily, I was paired with Eddie, the one guy on the team who was bigger than me.

I watched Will fighting it out with Little Murph. Will was fast and had the best hands on the team, but he wasn't too tough. I wondered if Coach Murphy had paired his kid up with Will on purpose? Murph quickly outmuscled Will, and beat our backup goalie Tyler five-hole. Lizzy O'Neil and Younyoung Lee were next. Lizzy was actually bigger than Younyoung, but Younyoung was pretty strong for a quiet kid, even if he didn't like to hit. They each got off shots which went wide before Tyler finally made a save on a Lizzy snap shot.

The year before, Lizzy had been the alternate. Everyone thought it was just because she was Coach O'Neil's niece, but I heard they had won more games when she was there than when she wasn't. She hustled as much as anyone on our team, as if she had something to prove every second. Being the only girl playing E Mass hockey as a Pee Wee Major, I can understand. She did have something to prove.

Ben and Billy battled it out next, followed by Sully and Bake. Woody was matched with Peter Donohue, our alternate, which was lucky for Woody. Peter knew more about hockey than anyone, but he just did not have that killer instinct on the ice. Woody beat him easily, yet Peter continued to smile. That was not surprising. Peter loved everything about hockey. He was the only kid I knew who got excited about suicides! Mac moved back into the goal, and Drew and Moose went next. They fought to a draw, and then it was Eddie and me.

The puck was dropped and bounced toward me. I pulled back my stick to blast a slap shot at Mac, but just as my wooden blade was ready to connect with the puck, slam! I was hit from behind and knocked flat onto the ice. Eddie picked up the loose puck and fired a slap shot into Mac's pads. As I was getting up off the ice, going for the rebound, Eddie's shoulder drilled me in the chest, and I was back down. Eddie blasted another big shot, but he misconnected. Instead of rocketing into the air, the puck dribbled on the ice. Mac looked caught by surprise, as the puck trickled between his skates. It was a perfect five-hole. Eddie raised his stick in triumph.

"Lucky," Drew muttered, a little too loudly from the cluster of kids waiting in line.

"What did you say?" Eddie said, glaring at his teammates.

"He said it was a lucky shot," Mac said from the goal.

"Luck?" Eddie shouted angrily, then suddenly broke into a huge grin. "That's the famous Germano fake! It fools them all the time."

"It fools you, too," one of the other boys said.

Eddie just grinned.

"Okay, boys, get some water," Coach Murphy said.

"You okay?" Eddie asked me in a friendly way.

"Yeah," I lied. My shoulder and hip killed, but I wasn't going to tell him that. "I just wasn't expecting a hit from behind. That's a penalty, you know."

"Not in practice, especially in the corner drill. Even in a game, they'll only call it when you slam a guy from behind into the boards, and even then only when he gets hurt. And you're not hurt." Eddie gave me a knowing smile.

I waited behind Lizzy and Sully for a drink. It was good to know all the names of the kids, at last. I wasn't the best at remembering people's names, but names of hockey kids stuck pretty well. We had been practicing for two weeks, and our first game was coming up that weekend! I couldn't wait. We were playing against the Junior Black Bears, which was supposed to be an average team in the league. If we wanted to go to Montreal, this was a team that we needed to beat.

Sully passed me a half-full water bottle, and I sprayed a mouthful through my face cage. When I was a Mite, I had always soaked myself whenever I tried that. As a Pee Wee, I could get most of the water into my mouth, and keep it there. I swallowed, and sprayed two more long squirts. It was warm and tasted a little metalic, but it was still good.

"You all right?" Ben asked me.

"Sure." I was feeling okay now.

"Eddie really nailed you. But you'll get him the next time."

I smiled.

"Maybe I'll just take it out on a few Black Bears on Saturday."

"That would be even better!" Ben said. "Hey, are you still able to drop me off on the way home today?"

"I asked my father. He said it would be okay. He finishes up after he does the next sheet of ice."

"Thanks."

"I also asked my mother if you could come over to my house after the game on Saturday. Can you?"

"I don't know," Ben said. "Probably. I'll ask my mother tonight. I'll tell you at practice tomorrow."

"Cool."

A whistle blew, and the coach directed the team to line up at the red line. The last two drills were shooting ones, and more fun. After practice, the boys were pretty quiet in the skate room. Everyone was exhausted. In no time, my father was at the door to our room, motioning me to come along. He then disappeared.

"Gotta go," I said to my teammates.

"Is that your father?" Mac asked.

"Yeah."

"Your father is the Zamboni guy?" he asked, laughing.

"Yeah," I said, and looked straight down at the ground. I was ashamed.

"He said that the other day," Moose said. "Didn't you hear?"

"Goalies live in their own world," Eddie said. "They don't hear nothing."

Silence followed. Mac looked as if he were trying to think of a clever comeback line, but he must have come up dry.

"I used to think that Zamboni guys were the coolest," Drew said. "I always said that if I couldn't play in the NHL or coach hockey, I would like to be a Zamboni driver."

"Me too," Mac said.

I smiled.

"Until I realized that a Zamboni guy is just a glorified janitor," Mac continued.

The other boys snickered nervously, with Will and Billy the only kids really laughing out loud. A wave of anger began to build in my chest.

"Hey, Mr. Breznikov does a great job doing the ice," Ben said.

"*Mister* Breznikov?" Billy asked. Billy was a good friend of Mac's. "Since when is Zamboni Brez *Mister* Breznikov?"

"They should call him 'mop and pail' Brez," Mac said. "He spends a lot more time on the floors than he does on the ice."

"Does he even know English?" Will said. I tried not to take it personally. Will pretty much criticized everyone. "I don't think so. I've ever heard him say a word."

"He probably knows the language better than you or me," Mac said. "Those Commie spies play dumb just so they can get more information when no one thinks they're listening."

A Commie spy? I wanted to hit Mac!

Suddenly, my father appeared again in the doorway.

"Hey!" he said, and angrily gestured me to come along.

I picked up my hockey bag and followed him. Ben came along behind.

"Papa, you remember Ben, right?" I asked just as we got to our old Ford station wagon.

My father nodded as he unlocked the trunk.

In a minute we were in the car and my father was driving toward the highway.

"You do a great job with the ice, Mr. Breznikov."

"You can call him Mr. Brez. He doesn't mind."

"I like the ice, Mr. Brez."

My father nodded, and continued driving. Once on the highway, he looked toward Ben, and asked, "Exit?" It sounded more like *exzeeeet.*

"Nineteen."

We traveled in silence for about five minutes. Once we were off the highway, Ben directed us to his house, which was about two minutes and one turn away.

"I'll see you tomorrow, Stas," Ben said. "Thanks for the ride, Mr. Brez."

"Don't forget to ask about Saturday night," I said. "Try to stay over."

Ben lugged his hockey bag along the front walkway and up the stairs to his porch. When he opened his front door, he waved to us and I waved back. The door shut, and we drove off.

"*So, when will you pass the puck?*" my father asked me in Russian.

"*I never had a chance!*" I answered in Russian, and then continued in English. "I pass when I am supposed to."

"*I don't mean you. The team! I see three of your practices in the last week, and I see no passing drill. Too little stick-handling, too. No break out drill. Just skate, shoot, hit.*"

"Yeah, but we're pretty good at those things."

"*To win at hockey, you must score, not hit. You boys can shoot the puck, but without passing and stick work, you will see few opportunities.*"

"Papa, it's just preseason. We've been together less than two weeks. Maybe Coach Murphy is just trying to get us is shape fast for the first game."

"Humph," he responded.

"You don't think so?"

"Stas," he said in English. "I hope you right."

Chapter 8

"There's no way we should be up by just one goal!" Coach Murphy yelled. "Those are the Taunton Jr. Black Bears! They're not the Junior Bruins or the Eagles. We're supposed to mop the ice with these guys!"

Mac smirked at me. *Mop the ice.* Was Mac making fun of my father?

Our burly coach glared at us. No one said a word back. I actually thought that we had played okay. The other team was pretty good! We were ahead 3-2, but we had two posts and Little Murph had missed a clean breakaway. With a break or two, it could just as easily have been 6-2, and Coach Murphy would be telling us how great we were playing.

Except maybe in the in-house and rec leagues, all coaches are like that. It really doesn't matter how you play. It's whether you win or lose.

"Boys," Coach Regan said calmly, "we have one more period to play. Let's do all the things we've worked on in practice."

Like what, I wondered? We skate hard and hit, plus shoot. We had been hitting really hard. We had had twice as many penalties as the Black Bears! And we had skated as hard as we could. We didn't have much chance to shoot, because the Black Bear defense was really good.

"Boys, let's punish them this period," Coach Murphy said.

"Yeah!" Eddie said.

"Yeah, yeah," the whole team cried.

"One, two, three..." Coach Murphy said quietly.

"Win!" the whole team hollered, and broke apart.

Billy, Little Murph and Sully were out on offense, with Eddie and Moose on defense. My line was next. I was playing right wing, with Ben on left and Lizzy at center. Our other line was Will, Younyoung and Bake. Bake was really Ted Bacon, but everyone just called him Bake.

The parents on both sides of the rink cheered encouragement to their teams as the boys lined up for the face-off to start the third period. Sully won the draw and dropped a pass to Moose, who dumped it up into the zone. Murph fought in the corner to gain control, but a Black Bear defenseman came up with the puck. He hit a perfect breakout pass to their center, who shot ahead, splitting our 'D'. The guy sprinted up ice.

Eddie pursued him, but wasn't fast enough. Their guy was flying! He went straight in on a breakaway. Mac skated out to meet him at the top of the crease. The Black Bear forward fired a wrist shot high to the stick side. Mac flicked his blocker up, and just caught a piece of the puck, deflecting it over the net.

"Yeah, Mac!" Woody hollered from the defensemen's end of the bench.

"Way to go!" Drew cheered.

"Good save!" I yelled, glad that Mac was my goalie. My town team had been good last year, but the goalie was a sieve, and we lost half our games just because of him. What a difference a goalie like Mac made. Even Tyler, our back-up goalie, was better than anyone in Braintree.

The puck went up and down ice twice more before Coach Murphy called for a line change. As Billy skated toward the bench, I hopped over the boards and was on the ice. Our opponents were skating it out of their own end, when Eddie broke up the play and dumped the puck back in again. I sprinted deep into the offensive zone, just trailing their defenseman who was racing toward the puck. We flew into the corner at almost the same time, except he beat me by a fraction of a second. I couldn't stop in time, and smashed him into the boards. The boy went down and the ref blew his whistle.

"Hitting from behind," the man in stripes said. "Two minutes in the box."

The guy I hit was slowly getting up, as the skaters from both teams tapped their sticks on the ice. The ref skated up to me, and directed me toward the penalty box.

"Hey, Number 2, you can't do that. You're lucky he's not hurt worse."

He's lucky, I thought. Besides, it wasn't intentional. Hockey's a tough game.

I stepped through the penalty box door, while the ref reported the infraction to the teenaged boy in a hooded sweatshirt who served as the official scorekeeper. I pulled the door shut and had a seat. I checked out my surroundings. Just the usual scuffed white boards and smudged glass. And then I noticed a PR carved into the bench. Did someone spend so much time in there that he needed to sign the bench, claiming it to himself? It was my second time there that game. How many more visits would I need before I felt entitled to mark that territory with my initials?

The sin bin. I smiled. I was a bad boy of hockey, sort of, and I liked it. I looked out on the action as the puck was dropped. The Black Bears controlled it, and instantly brought it up ice. Ben and Lizzy, along with Woody and Drew, formed a perfect four-corner box, while the Black Bears passed it around, trying a set up a good shot.

We gave them two outside slappers, which Mac stopped easily, but we couldn't get the puck out of our zone. Suddenly, their left wing skated across the crease, and was hit with a perfect pass from behind the net. He one-timed it, firing hard and low. Mac was just moving away from the post, when he lunged, trying to deflect the puck, but the far side of the net was open, and the puck slid in. The Black Bears had tied it up.

I was sick! The ref let me out of the penalty box, and muttered, "Smart penalty, huh?"

I gave him a dirty look but kept my mouth shut. Coach Murphy called for a line change, so I missed the whole shift, practically! Coach Murphy didn't say anything to me. Was the goal my fault? I felt terrible.

As the game continued, we began to really dominate, but their goalie stood on his head, stopping everything in sight. I had a slap shot from in close, and he made a 'look what I found' save. That means that he never saw the thing, and flashed his glove out in desperation, and the puck just luckily went right in.

With a minute to play, we pulled our goalie, and the coach put me out as a sixth skater. I got two more shots, but their goalie made the saves. The game ended in a tie.

The Black Bear kids were celebrating, while my team hung their heads low. It's always clear who should have won a tie game. Just look at the reactions of the kids when it's over. One team acts as if they won while the other thinks they lost.

We lined up, shook hands, and headed to our own skate rooms.

"Nice penalty," Mac said to me, as we stepped off the ice.

"Nice save," I shot back.

The post-game lecture was not as bad as I expected. Coach Murphy told us that we needed to win most of the next twelve games if we wanted to go to Montreal. He said that we needed to skate harder and hit harder. I thought that we skated and hit plenty hard. The puck just didn't go into the net.

When the coaches left, none of us said a word. It felt a little awkward, but I wasn't about to say anything. I was the first one packed and dressed, and just sat waiting for Ben, who was coming home with me.

"Good game, Stas," Eddie said as Ben and I got up to leave.

"Yeah, you did a great job in the box," Mac said.

"I was only there twice," I said.

"And it was only the tying goal they scored while you were there," Mac said.

"And I was in the bin for the first goal," Eddie said. "Are you going to blame that on me?"

Mac and Eddie stared at each other.

"Eddie," Mac said, "I blame you for every mistake this team makes. After all the time we've spent with you, your intelligence is starting to rub off on us all."

"That's all right, I'll send you the tutoring bill," Eddie said, and grinned.

I left with Ben and met my father outside by the snack bar. Ben walked to a vending machine, and bought a blue sports drink. My father handed me a water bottle filled with my green sports drink made from a powder. I squirted some into my mouth. It wasn't that cold, but it tasted great, and it cost almost nothing with the huge boxes of mix my mother bought at Save-All.

"We almost won, Papa," I said.

"*How can you-*" he began in Russian.

"English?" I asked, looking to see who was within earshot. Lots of people were nearby, but the noise level was pretty high with the crowds of people coming and going. Probably no one had heard him.

"How can you win with just dump and chase?" Papa said. "That not how to play! I do not see one good pass."

"But we outshot them!"

"Man for man, every one of you be better than every one of them. You faster and stronger, but they be smarter. They not have many shots, but beat you in *good* shots." The word *good* sounded more like *goot.*

Ben walked back to my father and me, joining us just as my mother, Yuriy and Katya stepped up to greet us.

"You guys should have won," Yuriy stated.

"Yeah," Katya said. "You had a lot more shots."

Yeah, but how many were *goot* shots, I wanted to ask. My father had taught me that it's not the *number* of shots that counts, but rather the number of *quality* shots. Did the Black Bears get more quality shots than we did, like my father said?

"Enough with hockey," my mother announced. "Let us go home."

Chapter 9

"Nice pass, Katya!" Ben said, tapping his tiny plastic stick to the carpet.

"Good shot," Katya said.

Yuriy turned around and reached into the knee hockey net, and pulled out the hard foam ball.

"Why don't we switch goals?" I asked.

"You have Yuriy, and I have your sister, Stas," Ben said. "You're the one who said that with the smaller net, it should even things out."

"Well, it's almost impossible to get the ball in that tiny thing, even with Katya as goalie."

"Maybe I'm just a better goalie than Yuriy," Katya said.

"Hah!" Yuriy said, and laughed.

"Maybe we should just stop playing," Ben said. "My knees are killing me."

I looked over at Ben's knees, and they were totally red. The hallway carpet was pretty rough, but Yuriy and I had built up callus on our knees from playing so much knee hockey.

"So Katya," Ben said, as he lay down his knee hockey stick, "do you play hockey too?"

"No, my father won't let me."

"Because you're too young?"

"No. Because I'm a girl."

"Really?" Ben said.

"They're making me do figure skating."

"That stinks."

"Yeah."

"Well, it would be cool if you ever made the Olympics," I said. "Those triple lutzes are pretty tough."

"It would be even cooler to play on an Olympic hockey team," Katya said, "and score a goal."

She had a point there.

"Do you want to watch a movie now?" I asked.

"Sure," Ben said.

We stepped into the living room, where my father was reading his Russian newspaper. He drove into Cambridge once a week to pick up a copy, and spent hours poring through it. He still pretty much thought of Russia as his home, and that newspaper kept him in touch with it.

I walked into the kitchen, where my mother was seated at the table, and I whispered to her, "Mama, do you think that we could watch a movie on TV?"

My mother glanced at my father sitting in his armchair in the living room, the only room that had a television.

"I don't know," she said.

"What is the matter? What do you have to whisper about?" my father asked in Russian.

"Nikolay," my mother said, "we have a guest. It is bad manners to speak in a language that he cannot understand."

"It's all right, Mrs. Brez," Ben said. "Next year, I'm going to take Russian in school. They don't start it until the seventh grade."

"They teach Russian at you school?" my father asked in English.

"Yeah," Ben said. "Everyone has to take a foreign language starting in grade seven. I'm going to take Russian because it sounds more interesting than the other languages. Plus, one of the Russian teachers is a hockey coach at the school."

"What is this name of school?"

"Meadows Prep," I said. "It's a private school. Mama said that maybe I can go there next year."

"If he works hard and earns a scholarship," my mother added.

"Russian in American school," my father said, and nodded his head. "In school in Russia, they all learn you the English. Some schools do more than others. Mine, no so good. I like Russian in American school. What you mean, scholarship?"

"Private school," my mother said, "it cost money. For some people, the school pays the bill. Most people, they are rich."

"Are you rich?" my father asked Ben.

"Nikolay!" my mother cried. "You not ask that!"

"That's all right," Ben said. "We're not rich. Just regular. We pay some tuition, but have a scholarship for the rest."

"Smart boy, huh?" my father asked.

"Not really," Ben said. "They give scholarships to a lot of the hockey players."

"Ah!" my father said. "They teach Russian and give scholarship to hockey players. That be good for my Stas." He paused, then looked back at me and continued, "So, what you whisper secret about?"

He looked back and forth, from me to my mother.

"The kids wanted to know if they could watch a movie," my mother said.

"*And move me from my chair*," he said in Russian. "What movie?" he asked, switching to English.

"Slap Shot," I said.

"You cannot watch Slap Shot!" my father said. "You too young. Language no good."

Slap Shot did have more four letter words than any other movie I had ever seen. But it was about hockey, and my father loved hockey. He had bought us Slap Shot for Christmas, but turned it off almost at the beginning. Yuriy and I knew where my father had hidden it, and when we were home alone, or with Katya, we would sometimes watch it.

"It be too late to watch movie anyway," my father said.

"Dad, it's Saturday night!" I cried.

"Yeah, it's Saturday night," Katya said.

"This be America. Do what kids want. Ugh! Okay, you watch movie, but no Slap Shot."

"Ben, what else do you want to see?"

"What other hockey ones do you have?"

"Mighty Ducks," I said, "D2, Mighty Ducks 3, Stanley Cup 2000, Wayne Gretzky, The Mario Lemieux story, The Greatest Fights in Hockey..."

"I love that one!" Ben cried. "Let's see that!"

"I love that one, too!" Katya said, and giggled. "Especially when they put the jerseys over the other guys' heads."

"Ugh," my father said, shaking his head. "Even my girl!"

"But Papa," I said, "you said that American hockey is not tough, like in Russia. You should *make* us watch the hockey fight video."

"Toughness, yes. No one be tougher than Russia. On Red Army team, they tough, but no fight. Fighting stupid."

"You used to watch the Red Army team in Russia?" Ben asked my father.

"Watch them?" I said, and then whispered to Ben. "He used to play for the Red Army team, back when they were the Soviet Union."

"Stas!" my mother cried, shooting me an icy glare. "Shh!"

"Did your father play in the Olympics?"

"No," I said quietly. "Not everyone on the Red Army team played Olympics, but he played with a lot of the guys who did play for the Soviet team. And his picture is in the Hockey Hall of Fame, with one of the teams that played against team Canada."

"Cool!" Ben said. "How come you never told me before?"

"He doesn't want us to tell people because he doesn't like people to ask him questions," Yuriy whispered. "If they did, he would have to answer."

"In English," I added in a hushed tone. "He hates to speak English because he's not very good at it, so he doesn't like people to know where he played."

My father was reading his paper, looking as if he didn't hear a word we were saying. Maybe he hadn't heard. He can zone out when he's reading the paper, especially when people are talking in English.

"Stop the secrets," Papa said without looking up from his paper.

"Mr. Brez, you speak real good English," Ben said.

"Yes, Nikolay," my mother said to my father, "and you would speak even better English if you return to the evening class."

"*Stop it!*" my father said in Russian as he pushed himself up out of his chair. "*I do not want to hear you tell me what to do. I am sick of it! And the boys, they talk about me like I'm not even here. I've had it! Just let the kids watch the movie.*"

My father glared at my mother and stormed out of the living room.

Chapter 10

"This is one practice I'm not looking forward to," Moose said as he pulled his laces as tightly as he could. My eyes went to the black hair on the back of his hands. Gorilla hands were what they looked like.

"I don't look forward to any practices," Will said, "except maybe the first couple of the season. I just like to play the games."

"Me, too," Eddie said. "Coaches never let me really hit guys in practice, but they love it when I kill a kid in a game." Eddie flashed that big grin of his, as he smacked his shoulder pads, exposing his large biceps.

"What about you, Younyoung?" Will asked.

Younyoung just shrugged his shoulders. I had never heard Younyoung Lee say a single word. I didn't even know what his voice sounded like! If the police ever asked me to identify his voice from a recorded phone call, I wouldn't be able to. That was pretty sad. All I knew about Younyoung was that he was Chinese or Japanese or something.

"Come on, Younyoung, tell us!"

Younyoung squirmed uncomfortably, avoiding eye contact with anyone.

"Let him be, Will," Woody said.

"Myself, I usually like practices," Peter said, snapping on his helmet. Peter Donohue was our alternate, and he had better like practices, because he'd hardly ever play in a game. Peter continued, "But I don't think I'll like this one very much."

"Why not?" Ben asked, looking up as he was tying his skates.

"Duh," Billy said, "Coach wasn't exactly thrilled that we blew that last game."

"Yeah," Bake said, "and against the Black Bears! They stink!"

"They don't really stink," Drew said. "They were a .500 team last year."

"Actually, they ended the season with a .475 winning percentage," Peter said. "Compared to the Sharks, that's poor."

"Thank you, professor," Will said. Peter had a photographic memory. He remembered about every statistic in the history of hockey, and so some of the kids called him 'professor.'

"And Coach Murphy expects us to go to Montreal," Bake said. "We can hardly lose a game if we want to go there. Two losses and we are virtually eliminated from the Cup."

"The Montreal Cup," Mac said, as he strapped on his leg pads. "I want that so bad, I can almost taste it."

"Me, too," Sully said, sitting on the bench, fully dressed except for his helmet. "And I heard that you get to stay with a French family. They're all French up there, French-Canadian."

"They do that so that parents won't mind letting their kids go," Woody said, "even if they have to miss a week of school. It makes it educational."

"Yeah, even Bake's parents will let him go," Will said. "They're both teachers, and never let him miss a day of school unless he's practically dead."

"I'm taking French in school," Bake said, not realizing that Will was making fun of him and his family, "so it really will help me."

"I take Supplemental English instead of French or Spanish," Eddie said, "so it won't help me."

"That's just reading class! That's the dummy class," Mac said, "for kids not smart enough for a foreign language."

"You're in there too," Eddie said.

"That's what I said," Mac said, "that's the dummy class. I'm a goalie! Goalies don't have to be smart. Just quick."

"Goalies and goons," Eddie said, and grinned. "I still want to go to Montreal, even if it won't help me in school."

I took reading, too, instead of a language. That was because English was still a new language for me, and I already knew a foreign language, Russian, even if it wasn't foreign to me. Actually, English was my foreign language.

"My family visited Toronto last year," Tyler said, "and we went to the Hockey Hall of Fame. They have the Montreal Cup on display there, with the team names of all the winners engraved on it."

"Wow!" I said. "That would almost be like being in the Hockey Hall of Fame!"

"Yeah," Tyler continued, "actually, we will be there if we win. Next to the Cup is a computer. You click on a year, and you see a roster of all the players on the winning team that year, along with tournament statistics and a picture."

"So if we win the Montreal Cup, our picture will be in the Hockey Hall of Fame?" I asked.

"Yup," Tyler said.

"Hey," Ben said, "your father is already in -"

"Ben!" I cried, scowling at my friend. He knew that my father didn't want anyone to know that he played hockey for the Red Army team.

"Sorry," Ben said.

"What are you talking about?" Sully asked.

"Nothing," I said.

"What's the big secret?" Mac asked. "What about your father?"

"Nothing!" I said angrily.

"It doesn't sound like nothing," Mac said.

"Hey, Mac," Ben said. "Let it rest."

"Something secret about Stas's father?" Billy asked. "There are no secrets on a team."

"Unless it's about the guy's double life," Mac said. "You know, Commie spy?"

"What?" I cried.

"Hey," Mac said. "if my old man was a Commie spy, I'd keep that a secret, even from my teammates. So that must be it."

"Cut it out, Mac," Ben said.

"If it's not that, then tell us," Mac said.

"I can't."

"So you're one of them, too?" Mac said to Ben. "That makes me sick. I guess I can't blame Stas, there. He was born a stinking Commie. He can't help it. It's in his blood. But you, Ben?"

"Mac," Woody said, "chill."

"And besides," Lizzy added, "Russia is not even a Communist country anymore."

I blinked in surprise. Lizzy had actually said something! It was one of the few things I had ever heard her say. She was almost as quiet as Younyoung!

"Yeah," Woody said, "so let's just think about the big game coming up."

"Big game?" Eddie said. "It's against Hartford. If we can't beat them, we can join the rec league. My old coach used to always tell us that we were playing like in-house mites whenever we lost. The funny thing is, the guy also coached an in-house mite team, and so I always wondered what he said to them when they lost."

"Probably that they were playing like Special Olympics kids," Will said.

"That's not funny," Younyoung said. Everyone looked at Younyoung, shocked that he had said anything. "My cousin plays Special Olympics hockey," he added in almost a whisper.

No one said a word.

"Sorry, man," Eddie said.

"What are you sorry for?" I asked. "You didn't say anything. Will did."

Everyone looked at Will, who started to fidget with the straps of his helmet.

"Hey," Will said, "I didn't mean anything bad. I didn't even know they had Special Olympics hockey."

"My older sister volunteers for Special Olympics hockey," Drew said. "It's a good program for those kids. And some of the kids are decent skaters."

"Hey, come on," Woody said, "let's forget about Special Olympics for now. Let's think about the game we're going to play."

"But it's just Hartford," Tyler said. "I might even get a chance to play in this one!" Backup goalies usually got to play against the lousy teams.

"The game is at Hartford," Woody said. "That's a long drive. It's hard to get going there. They've jumped on some pretty good teams in the first period and held on. Hartford is never easy in their own rink."

The door opened and Coach Murphy and Coach Regan walked into the room. Everyone was instantly quiet.

"Was that laughter I heard?" Coach Murphy asked sternly.

No one said a word.

"After that last game, someone dares to laugh?"

More silence.

"You guys played like a town team against the Black Bears!" Coach Murphy said.

Most of the guys looked at Eddie, who was trying to suppress a grin.

"Is that funny?" Coach Regan asked. "Eddie, do you want to go back to your town team?"

Eddie's smile disappeared quickly. He shook his head no.

"Boys, it's a privilege to play Triple-A hockey," Coach Regan said, "especially in this league. You are playing with and against the best. The best of the best. Play like you belong here."

"And that means skate hard and play physical," Coach Murphy said. "Those Black Bears still skated with zip in the third period. If we pounded them harder, they'd have had nothing by the third, and no way would they have come back like they did."

But they would not have gotten two of their goals if we hadn't been in the penalty box. Two of their goals were power plays goals. I wasn't about to mention that to Coach Murphy, though.

Coach Murphy dropped his voice, and spoke very seriously.

"I'm going to work you hard this practice. It's not to punish you. It's to toughen you up. I want you to feel no pain in the next game. I want it to be a walk in the park, compared to this practice. And I want you to know the consequence of poor play, and remember that at Hartford this weekend."

Boy, it sure did sound like a punishment that we were getting. I wanted to ask what a punishment was if it wasn't this, but I figured it was wiser to keep my mouth shut.

"Let's go, boys," Coach Murphy said. He stood and headed out to the ice, with Coach Regan next to him. The whole team nervously followed.

After a few laps of forward and backwards skating, the coaches lined us up along the boards.

"We'll start with suicides," Coach Murphy announced. "Back and forth ten times. If you do not come to a full stop, you owe me twenty pushups. If you're in the last five, you owe me thirty pushups. If you're last, you owe me fifty pushups. Got it?"

"Do goalies count?" Tyler asked.

That's a good question, I thought. They were always last in skating drills.

"Just skate!" Coach Murphy yelled, as he blew his whistle without answering the question.

I skated hard. I did not want to do extra push-ups. I hated push-ups. And I hated when coaches made us race against our teammates like this. Some guys were just faster than others. I was one of the slower guys, just because I was big. But I was determined not to end out in the bottom five. If they counted goalies, I could probably avoid those extra push-ups.

I stopped sharply on my left edges, and pushed off quickly, heading back to the other boards. By the third stop and start, my legs began to tire. Still, seven more times to go! Ugh! I didn't know if I could make it. These coaches were crazy. But I dug down and pushed off as hard as I could. The other kids were getting tired, too. It was going to be a long practice.

Chapter 11

The radio crackled. The reception was breaking up. I hid the trace of a smile which was starting to form at the edges of my mouth. We were almost out of range for the stupid Russian radio station that my father always listened to. It was a Boston station, and the signal wasn't too strong. I prayed that there was not a Russian station in Hartford.

I didn't like my father to listen to that station, but it was just because I liked to listen to my own station, which I guess would be called soft rock. My mother and sister liked that station, too. Yuriy liked sports talk radio the best, but he hardly ever got to hear it in the car, unless he really whined to my mother and made her feel guilty.

That day, though, not only did I have to listen to that stupid Russian music, but poor Ben had to listen to it, too. We were taking Ben to the game in Hartford, which was about a two hour ride from home. Personally, I thought it was kind of rude to play something on the radio which some people in the car couldn't understand. When I had said that to my father once, he said that people were lucky to be getting a ride. When he was a boy, he had to walk a mile to catch a bus to the rink, lugging a heavy hockey bag the whole way, often in bitter cold weather. My father still laughed at the American hockey parents who carry their kid's hockey bag from the car to the skate room.

Suddenly, a Russian polka, or whatever it was, boomed crystal clear out of the car radio. My father smiled. We were in the midst of a long incline on the Mass Pike, and whenever our car went up a hill, the reception became clearer. But I would be smiling soon. It always got worse when we drove down on the other side. I eyed the top of the hill up ahead. The reception would change soon.

Ben was just listening to his own music through headphones on his CD player. I badly wanted one of those portable CD players, but they cost too much money. Any extra money went to our hockey. I made some money shoveling snow in the winter and mowing lawns and delivering papers in the summer, but I needed to spend all of that on hockey equipment. My parents did give me equipment, but it was either my father's old stuff, or it was second hand. If I wanted newer, nicer hockey gear, I had to buy it myself. My skates were getting pretty small, and I wanted a new pair of 606 Jets, which cost more than $300, and that was a sale price. I was hoping for a blizzard or two to help me earn the money for them. I had already saved $150. I was almost halfway there.

As we approached the top of the long hill on the highway, I prayed that the Russian radio station would fade on the other side. Sure enough, as we headed down, the music was completely drowned out by staticky interference.

"Can I change the station?" I asked my father, trying not to sound too eager.

"*Isn't it better that you think of your game?*" he answered in Russian.

"Papa, when it is just us," I whispered, "I don't mind if you speak in Russian. But can't you use English when I have a friend with me?" I nodded toward Ben in the back seat, who had his eyes shut while his head bobbed up and down to the rhythm of hip hop.

"Your friend is not with you. He is in his own world, listening to his own music. He would not know if I speak Russian or Greek or English."

"He had to listen to his own music. He's not into Russian waltzes," I said, and then added sarcastically, "like I am."

"Listen to what you like," he said with disgust, turning the radio to a random station, which happened to be playing classic rock, not exactly my first choice, but better than Russian music. *"It is your game. Winning or losing does not matter to me. It should matter to you, and not to me. You are old enough to decide."*

"Papa, it's Hartford we're playing. They stink!"

"You said that about the Black Bears. You did not win that game."

"We totally outplayed them!" I said, slipping into Russian the way I sometimes did, especially when I got mad.

"But you did not pass the puck in the offensive zone. Everyone just skated and shot slap shots, from far out, from bad angles. You got very few quality shots. And I watched you practice this week. Where was the passing? Where was the defense? Your coach, he skates you hard, yes, and that is good. But skating and shooting is all he does."

That *was* pretty much all we did at practice. Early in the season, I just assumed that the coaches were trying to get us in shape after the summer, but practices had not changed much since then. Still, everyone did skate hard for our coaches. While Coach Murphy yelled a lot, and he was a little scary, he did joke around, too, and made me feel good when I did something well, which was usually hitting.

"Papa, what were your practices like on the Red Army team?" I asked, switching back to English.

"We skated hard, like you do, but always skated with the puck."

"But skating with the puck slows you down, doesn't it? Can't you skate harder and get in better shape without a puck?"

"At first, but eventually the puck, it becomes part of you. You skate with it as easily as you skate with the stick in your hands."

"That probably works if you're already on the Red Army team. But what about Youth Hockey?"

"*When I was your age, I played for Spartak, a hockey club in Moscow. We practiced just as I did later with the Red Army team. Always with the puck.*"

"If the Sharks did that, we'd spend the whole practice slowing up to chase pucks in the corner."

"*No,*" my father said in Russian, "*there were always many pucks on the ice. If you lose a puck, you do not slow up at all. Just pick up an extra one when you can. Usually, half the practice was skating and stick-handling. After that, we pass and shoot, mostly passing. We did breakouts and weaves and drops. Our passing, it was a thing of beauty.*"

"I bet you had a good power play," I said.

"Spartak? The best," he said in English, and smiled. "Pass, pass, pass, pass, break to the goal, pass, shoot. Ah! Gorgeous!"

Listening to him, I was a little jealous. While I loved all the shooting we did, especially the slap shots, those passing drills did sound pretty cool. Zipping along the highway, we both became lost in our thoughts. A little while later, I did notice that Ben had taken off his headphones and was listening to our car radio. Classic rock was still on. I hadn't bothered changing the station. I was mostly thinking about hockey, hockey in America and hockey in Russia. Thinking about what my father had said, I almost wished that I was back in Moscow playing for Spartak, or Demano or ZSKA.

But other than hockey, life was much better in America. Better house. Better food. More fun things to do, if you had the money anyway. Someday, I thought, I'd have a lot of money. The NHL pays pretty good. The Bruins were always losing their star players because they went somewhere else to make millions of dollars more. I figured that I'd stay in Boston, though, even if I made a few million less. Boston was a good hockey town. The fans liked big strong players who could hit, and that was me.

We drove the rest of the trip in silence. I saw Ben nod off a few times. I just thought about hockey. It seemed that in no time at all, we were off the highway. My father grabbed the directions that my mother had rewritten in Russian for him. He made a few turns and then grumbled something about whether South Street was the same as South Road. He made a turn, complained about the terrible directions, turned around, made two more turns and then suddenly, there before us stood a huge domed rink.

"You play smart," my father said in English, as I got out of the car.

I nodded and smiled at him. I appreciated that he did speak in English.

"Thanks for the ride, Mr. Brez," Ben said.

I opened the trunk and pulled out my hockey bag and sticks. Ben did the same.

"This should be fun," he said as we headed for the rink.

Chapter 12

I was starting! My blood pumped hard through my veins as I skated toward center ice with linemates, Ben and Lizzy. Eddie and Moose were starting on defense. I was a starting forward for the South Shore Sharks, an Eastern Mass hockey team!

As the refs were conferring with the official scorekeeper, I was thinking back to the day I made my town's Squirt A team. The coach had gathered us together after the tryout, and described us as *la crème de la crème*, which he told us meant 'the best of the best.' Of all the nine and ten year-olds playing hockey in Braintree, the fourteen of us were the tops. We would play against the best each town had to offer in the very tough South Shore Hockey League. Now, two years later, there I was, on a team with the best kids from all of those town A teams, and I was starting. Coach Murphy picked our line because he said that we had been skating really aggressively. I was determined to show him how well he chose.

The ref skated toward the face-off circle while I leaned down on my stick and stared at my opposing wing. He was a head shorter than I was, and he did not glance at me. He was afraid, I was sure.

The ref dropped the puck, and just as Lizzy put her stick on it, I slammed into my opposing wing, and the ref instantly blew his whistle.

"Number 2, that's interference," the short man in black-and-white stripes said to me. "Take a rest."

He escorted me to the box, and then skated over to the scorekeeper's booth, and gave the penalty information to the guy in there. I looked up at the clock. 14:59. One second into the game! I wondered if that was some sort of record. Part of me thought it was funny, but another part of me was mad because I would miss my whole first shift.

I sat back and watched the game. Hartford tried to control the play in their offensive zone, but never got more than two passes off before one of our guys intercepted the puck and sent it down the length of the ice. We switched lines after a minute, and Billy and Little Murph, along with Woody and Drew did just as good a job of penalty killing. By the time my penalty was over, our third line was on the ice, and my line was due out next. At 12:59, I opened the door of the penalty box and I sprinted back to our bench. Bake hopped into play as I stepped off the ice.

"Nice job," Coach Murphy said. "You showed them what they were up against. They're all playing scared, now."

I smiled. Coach Regan stepped over and patted me on the shoulder. On the ice, we were dominating. Hartford couldn't get the puck out of their zone. Eddie fired three nasty slap shots, but two went over the net and the third went right into the goalie's chest. We changed on the fly, and I was back out on the ice.

We had dumped the puck into the zone, and their defenseman was skating it out when I approached the play. I accelerated and slammed into their puck-handler. I bounced off him, flying up in the air, hitting the ice flat on my back. The other kid went down, too. Ben picked up the loose puck and sprinted toward the goal when the ref whistled offsides. My four teammates skated to me, and touched gloves with me as I pushed myself up.

"Nice hit," Lizzy said.

"Way to go," Woody said.

We lined up for the face-off just outside the blue line. Lizzy won it. We dumped the puck into the zone, and I chased their defenseman who was skating into the corner to pick up the puck. As soon as he touched it, I slammed into him, and the kid crashed headfirst into the boards, falling to the ice. The whistle blew.

The boy didn't move. A hush hung over the arena. I held my breath. I wanted to punish him, but I didn't want to kill him. Three Hartford coaches sprinted onto the ice and surrounded the fallen skater. The silence in the rink was eerie. The only movement in the stands was a woman running down from the bleachers and up to the glass, standing as close as she could get to the injured boy. From the panicked look on her face, I knew it had to be the kid's mother. She didn't take her eyes off her son. Her pain was too much for me to look at, and I pulled my eyes away from her. Instead, I looked back to the kid on the ice. Finally, about thirty seconds later, the boy's leg moved a little. Whew!

"Hitting from behind," the ref called out as the boy got up to the sound of applause and the tapping of sticks. The ref skated right up to me and said, "You know the routine."

I was back in the box. It was starting to feel like home. I didn't know if I liked that. Fortunately, the Hartford Devils could not mount much of an attack on their power play. In the closing seconds, Billy picked off a pass, and split their pinching defensemen at the points. He sprinted the length of the ice, and went in alone against their big goalie. The Hartford goaltender came way out of the net, totally removing any shooting angle. Even though Billy was completely alone and didn't have to hurry, he did not slow down at all. As the goalie was sliding backwards toward the net, Billy faked right and pulled the puck left, and slid it across the red line and into the net. A short-handed goal! We were ahead, 1-0.

Five seconds later, I was out of the box and sprinting back to my bench. Sully hopped over the boards and onto the ice as I approached. The coaches both gave me fives as I took my position with Ben and Lizzy. Billy's line was still on the ice. Little Murph picked up a loose puck in the neutral zone and instantly hit Billy with a perfect pass as he was streaking down the right wing. Billy deked their left defenseman and flew toward the net while the Devil center desperately backchecked. Billy fired a shot from the face-off circle, which the goalie deflected with his blocker. Little Murph was on the rebound, and he fired at the net. The big Devil goalie kicked it out. Billy had his skates planted in the low slot, waiting for the rebound, when, wham! Down he went!

The ref blew the whistle.

"Cross checking!" he said. "Two minutes."

Billy slowly dragged himself up off the ice.

"That was intentional!" Coach Murphy screamed.

"Intent to injure!" one of the Shark parents angrily yelled from the stands.

The refs ignored the angry coaches and fans, and calmly escorted the Devil player, Number 22, to the penalty box.

"22, when he gets out of the box, rip his head off," Coach Murphy said to me.

"What about me, coach?" Eddie said. "I'll get him."

"We only have four 'D'. Stas can do it."

I smiled nervously. I didn't know whether to feel proud that he chose me or insulted that he could afford to have me in the box.

"Ben's line, get out there!" Coach Murphy said.

Lizzy, Ben and I skated out for the face-off in the offensive zone. We were on the power play! The puck was dropped, and Ben controlled it, instantly shuffling it back to Moose at the point. Moose pulled his stick back and ripped a slap shot. The puck stayed low, and the Devil goalie kicked it out with his left pad. The rebound shot right out to me. I one-timed it back to the net. The goalie was still sliding across the crease when the puck slid into the net. Goal! I had scored! My first goal as a Shark!

I raised my stick in celebration while my teammates surrounded me, all raising their gloves to me. I tapped each glove, and returned to my position at center ice. I saw the Devil, Number 22, skate out of the penalty box and go over to his coach. He then skated to center ice, where he would take the face-off. I looked back to my bench, and saw Coach Murphy subtly nod at me. I nodded back. This was my chance.

We won the face-off, and Woody dumped the puck into the offensive zone. Lizzy chased the puck into the left corner while I watched their Number 22, who covered Ben in front of the goal. Lizzy won the battle for the puck in the corner, and flipped it in front of the goal. The goalie deflected it, steering it behind his net. Number 22 sprinted to the left of the net to get it while I raced around the right side of the goal to get there. Approaching the puck from opposite directions, I saw Number 22 lower his head. I accelerated and raised my left elbow, smashing into him as he touched the loose puck.

Whack! My elbow caught his lower facemask, and the Devil forward seemed to leave his feet before landing flat on his back on the ice. He instantly curled into a ball, his howls of pain drowning out the whistles of the referees. The high pitched whistles finally rose above the boy's wails, and we stopped skating.

Number 22's legs were kicking as he yelled. I felt terrible. At least he was moving. He'd be okay. The Hartford coaches ran out onto the ice and surrounded their injured player. I stood frozen, about ten feet from the downed skater.

"Back to the bench," Lizzy said to me, pulling me away and guiding me toward our signaling coach.

All of our players were staring at the screaming Devil player. I was imagining that it was me who was hurt and in pain like

that, thanking God that it was someone else. I'm sure that all
the other Sharks were thinking something like that, too. We
gathered around our coaches. Number 22 wouldn't stop
screaming. I wanted to cry.

"Stas, you did exactly what you were supposed to do," Coach
Murphy said. "That kid is twice the size of Billy, and you saw
what he did to him. He's not so tough against someone his own
size, is he?"

Looking at Number 22 still writhing in pain, although a little
more quietly, I didn't feel so hot about what I had done.

We stood there for about ten minutes when at last the sound
of an ambulance rang from outside the rink. Seconds later, two
EMTs slid across the ice pushing a stretcher toward the injured
player. They examined Number 22, looking mostly at his right
knee. Finally they put the kid on the stretcher. As they rolled
him off the playing surface, all the players tapped their sticks to
the ice while the parents cheered.

The ref skated to our bench and said to Coach Murphy,
"Number 2, elbowing, intent to injure. He's done for the game."

Done? I was done for the game? That wasn't fair! It was just a
check! If he hadn't dropped his head, I would have gotten him in
the shoulders! Everyone used elbows when they checked!
Besides, I didn't touch his knee. He must have twisted it when
he fell.

"Let's go," the ref said to me, leading me toward to door.

"Yeah!" I heard a mother scream from the seats behind the
Devil bench. "Get him out of here! He shouldn't play again!"

"Good work, ref!" a father yelled.

"Get the thug outta here!" another mother jeered.

"Kill him!" a father screamed.

My head hung low as I skated out the door and walked
across the black mat toward our skate room. I entered and sat
in there alone, slowly taking off all my equipment. I didn't know

whether I was allowed to go out and watch the rest of the game from the stands, or whether the ref would see me and kick me out of the rink. I didn't want to leave, and so I just sat alone on the hard wooden bench, in my street clothes, and listened to the sound of hockey outside.

I heard the puck bang against boards, then came lots of cheering. Cheers and bangs. That's all I heard. It was clear when there was a goal, because the noise got to be the loudest then. Or maybe the fans were applauding a great save. I had no idea who was winning. I hoped that it was our team. Mostly I was wishing that I could be playing. I sat alone in the skate room, surrounded by gray cinderblock walls spotted with hanging street clothes. Empty Shark hockey bags littered the floor. It was torturous, listening to the action, but not being able to play. I thought about Number 22, and decided that he was worse off than I was. Not only was he in a lot of pain, but it would be a long time before he would play again. I'd probably be suspended for one game, and then be back on the ice.

Waiting for this game to end was about the longest hour of my life.

Chapter 13

"You guys rose to the occasion," Coach Murphy said. "You skated hard, you hit hard, and you won."

My teammates all smiled. I began to smile myself, even though I hadn't done much.

"This was a game where each one of you guys contributed," the coach continued in his strong Boston accent. "Tyler made some nice saves in that third period. Mac did the job in the first two periods. An impressive combined shutout. Good job."

The boys all looked toward Mac and Tyler, and nodded to them in appreciation.

"You know, I've been around this sport a long time, and I can tell you that hockey games can turn on a dime. Stas did not spend a lot of time on the ice for us, but he set the tone in the few minutes he did skate. He intimidated the Devils, making everything we did all day that much easier. If we play like that all season, we will win. I'm not a big 'game puck' kind of guy, but the tone he set sparked this team to its first season win, and I'd like to give Stas the game puck."

Coach Murphy stepped over to me and handed me a puck. The other boys clapped. Even Mac was clapping lightly! Feeling confused and surprised, but still pretty good, I took the puck and mumbled a word of thanks to my coach.

"Practice on Monday, boys," Coach Murphy said. "Nice work."

"Good job," Coach Regan said, and both coaches walked out of the skate room.

"Yeah!" Eddie screamed. "Yeah! Where are we going?"

There was a moment of quiet, and then Drew said, "Home?"

"Montreal!" Eddie yelled. "This win is the first step to Montreal!"

I smiled. Montreal. The Monteal Cup. Maybe, just maybe, we would go to Montreal, and win. Just going would be unbelievable, but to win, and make the Hockey Hall of Fame, well, that would be a dream come true. A dream of a lifetime.

The score had been 10-0, a decisive win, a win that proved something.

Piece by piece, the guys began to remove their clothing and equipment. Their jerseys all came off almost at once. For a second, with Shark game shirts over their heads, they looked like a gang of headless horsemen. Next came the ripping of velcro, as elbow pads and shoulder pads were torn off. And for the first time, I was almost grossed out by the 'hockey odor.' Hockey odor comes from sweat, saturated in clothing that rarely gets washed and in pads that never get washed. The stink festers and multiplies inside closed hockey bags. Left overnight, it pretty much dries up or sinks deep into the equipment, and is mostly released when combined with new sweat after a practice or game.

At that moment, I almost wanted to gag. I wondered why the stink had never grossed me out before? Probably because when I played, it was my own smell, and no one is ever grossed out by their own smells, whether it's sweat odor or other kinds.

"Did you score any goals?" I asked Ben, who was taking off his shin pads on the bench next to me.

"One," Ben said. "Billy got a hat trick, and Eddie and Moose each had slap shot goals from the point. Little Murph got two, and I'm not sure whether Will or Younyoung got the last one. It was a rebound goal, and they were both hacking at it."

"Youn got it," Bake said. Youn was Younyoung. Some of the kids called him Youn for short.

"Nice job," I said, turning left to Younyoung, who was carefully placing his skates in his plain black bag. He was the only kid besides me who didn't have a fancy Shark bag.

Younyoung smiled and looked away quickly.

"Thank you," he whispered.

He was so shy! He looked like a really nice kid, but he was so hard to get to know.

"Yeah," Bake said, "it was a good second effort goal. Youn looked good out there, with a ton of awesome passes. And Eddie had some crushing checks."

"Yeah," Eddie said, flexing his muscles. "And Sully flattened a kid who was hacking at Mac. Sully, he's the man."

Eddie ripped away a long string of clear tape from around his shin pads, squeezed it in his right hand, and whipped the tiny ball of tape at Sully. It hit Sully on the side of the head. Sully picked it up, and threw it back at Eddie. Eddie very coolly caught the tape ball right in front of his face, and smiled a big, toothy grin.

"Why, thank you, Sully," Eddie said. "That was a two tape ball hit you made in the game. Thanks for giving me the tape back."

Eddie reared back to throw the ball of tape back at Sully. Mac, sitting near Sully, turned to the side and shielded his face. Eddie stopped mid-throw.

"Look at our goalie," Eddie said. "Afraid! Afraid of a stinking ball of tape! Hah!"

Mac put down his hand and Eddie threw the tape ball and hit him just above the waist.

Mac looked down at his stomach. He slowly raised his head and stared at Eddie. The room instantly quieted.

"Do you know what you almost hit?" Mac asked, speaking slowly. "Six inches lower, and you would be in big trouble."

"Six inches lower and *you* would be in big trouble," Eddie said, and everyone laughed. "With that monster goalie cup of yours, something must be awfully precious down there."

"With you on 'D', Eddie, I need all the protection I can get."

'What are you talking about, Mac? You hardly touched the puck today."

"That's true," Tyler, our backup goalie, said. "They even let me into the game."

"Hey, you made a few nice saves," Mac said.

"Yeah, Tyler," a few other kids said. Tyler wasn't as good as Mac, and probably wouldn't play in a close game all season, but he was a nice guy, and all the kids liked him. They all felt bad for him, too. What fun is it when the only time you play is when your team is way ahead. But a team needs two goalies for practice, and needs a spare in case the first string goalie gets hurt. Everyone knew that it was important to keep Tyler feeling good about being a Shark.

"Give Tyler the tape," Woody said.

Someone tossed the tape ball to Tyler, who began unraveling it, and then started to wrap it around his ball, which was about the size of a softball. Coach Regan had said that they didn't want any tape or trash left in any skate room, after practices or games, and had suggested that someone collect any old hockey tape and make one big ball with it. By the end of the season, it might be as big as a medicine ball! Tyler had volunteered to be the tape ball man. I wondered how big the ball of tape would really get.

The guys continued to joke around. Coach Regan stuck his head into the skate room, and said, "Let's go, guys! It's a long ride to Boston, and a lot of the parents are itching to go."

I liked being a Pee Wee, because parents didn't come into the skate room any more after games. The kids could have a lot more fun, and they weren't rushed as much. Some first year Pee Wees didn't like that they had to tie their own skates, but by second year, no one would even think of having a parent tie them. They just enjoyed having their parents stay away. My first practice with the Sharks, I had been worried that the guys would act differently because we had a girl with us, but I don't think it mattered. Lizzy said almost nothing, and we all pretty much forgot she was a girl. She played like a guy, and that was what counted. I was just glad that I had switched from tightie-whities to boxers over the summer. I would have been embarrassed to have her see me in my old underwear. Boxers were cool, though.

The kids stuffed the last of their equipment into their bags, and headed out.

"Nice game, Stas," Little Murph said as he left.

"Yeah, nice game," Bake said.

Billy nodded to me as he passed me, and Mac followed, and gave me a nod as well. I couldn't believe it! I had hardly played, but all the kids thought I did a great job. Younyoung Lee walked toward me with his eyes down, but just as he passed, he glanced up and smiled. He might have whispered, "Good game," but I wasn't sure. Still, he had smiled and said something to me! That was a first for Younyoung.

I was beaming as I walked out of the skate room, and into the lobby. I looked for my father in the crowd of adults. I recognized most of the Shark parent faces, but still hadn't connected all the parents to their kids yet. There was a big group of Shark adults clustered together, drinking coffee and laughing, but my father was not with them. I knew he wouldn't be. He didn't like to talk to anyone, not in English anyway.

My eyes searched the busy lobby and concession area, and I finally spotted him by the door to the rink, watching the game on the ice. I shuffled my way across the crowded room to him.

"Papa, I'm ready."

"*What took so long?*" he said in Russian. "*You didn't have to get dressed. You had an hour to do that during the game.*"

"We won, though. That was good, right?"

"*Humph. That Devil team, your town team could have beaten them. A waste of time. And you, you did nothing.*"

"Papa, I got the game puck!" I said, reaching into my bag to show him.

"*That's foolish!*"

"No, really. The coach said that my hitting made the other team scared."

"*Your coach must not have seen the same game I did, or he does not know hockey. Scared or not, with your team's talent, you should easily win against Hartford. Your hit meant nothing, except to the boy who will lose half his season because of you.*"

I swallowed hard. I had forgotten about that poor kid. He was probably at the hospital right now. Maybe he just had a bruise, but I didn't think so. At that moment, Ben walked up to us, a large sports drink in hand. I was thirsty, too, but didn't say anything to my father. I had forgotten to bring my water bottle full of sports drink mix. My father just turned around and walked out of the rink and to our car. Ben and I followed.

Chapter 14

Up the ice. Down the ice. About one hundred little kids were skating in a pack. When the instructor whistled, they went one way, and then at the next whistle, they went the other way. And that's about all they did. I wasn't paying too much attention to any of the details of the drills, like what edges they were using. I was just mesmerized by the incredible mix of colors swarming over the ice. The kids had on bike helmets and hockey helmets of every design and color you could think of. Combined with their bright winter jackets and snow pants, the crowded ice surface was like an animated, swirling work of art.

Then I spotted Katya's purple bicycle helmet. She looked bored stiff. The only time she smiled was when she skated toward the goal, or actually, to where the goal should have been. They put away the real nets for figure skating. When Katya approached the crease, she pretended to hold a hockey stick, and deked one invisible defenseman and fired a pretend shot to the far corner. It must have gone in because she raised her hands over her head and beamed. She actually made a pretty good move. Maybe she *would* make a good hockey player. Too bad she would never have a chance. My father thought that there was no way that a girl should ever play hockey. It was too rough. Katya had argued that girls do not check, but my father refused to listen. Watching the beginner figure skaters, I felt bad for Katya. Man, did it look boring!

I glanced back at the clock. 4:30. The little kids were off the ice in twenty minutes, and I would be on at five o'clock. My father had signed her up for the Hingham lessons instead of the ones in Braintree because they usually came just before our practice, and I think he might have gotten a discount, too, for working at the rink. Katya didn't like that, because all her friends from school skated at Braintree. She didn't know one other kid at Hingham.

"What are you watching?" a girl's voice asked from behind me.

I turned around. It was Lizzy.

"Oh, hi, Lizzy. I'm just watching my sister."

"You have a sister? Which one?"

"That one there, with the blue jacket and purple helmet."

"Really?" Lizzy said. "I was just watching her. I saw her deke a goalie and score!"

Lizzy smiled at me and I smiled back.

"Yeah, that's her," I said.

"She's a good skater," Lizzy said. "How many years has she skated?"

"This is her first year," I said.

"Wow, then she's really good! How come she doesn't play hockey instead?"

"My father. He thinks that hockey is too rough for girls."

"But she can play girls hockey. It's not like the game we play."

"My father doesn't know that. He's pretty old fashioned."

"I'll invite your sister to play with my family sometime. My father teaches at Meadows Prep, and my whole family plays shinny when there's free ice there."

"That sounds cool!"

"It is. That's where I learned to skate. I was the youngest. My four older brothers played, plus my mother and father play, so they dragged me on the ice when I was two so they all could play and no one would have to watch me off the ice. I'll definitely ask your sister to join us next time we play. What's her name?"

"Katya."

"Pretty name," Lizzy said. "Hey, and you can play, too."

Awesome! I beamed but didn't say anything.

"Hey," Lizzy said, "gotta go get ready." She lowered her voice and added sarcastically, "You know, girls are so slow getting dressed. See you in there."

I nodded. My father was in the lobby, emptying trashcans. I knew that I should have been heading to our skate room, getting dressed for practice, but I did not want to cross the lobby while my father was there, especially when he was emptying the trash. He was like a janitor! No one wants to be the kid of the janitor. When I was little, I thought that the Zamboni driver was about the coolest person alive. That was in Russia, and my father did not drive a Zamboni there. He worked in a factory. But if he did drive one then, I would have bragged about it to my friends. As you get older, though, you start to see a Zamboni driver as just a guy who works at a rink. Maybe Mac was right, they are only glorified janitors. I hated that my father worked at the rink I played at, especially because he never said a word to anyone. People must have thought that he was as dumb as dirt. But dumb was better than being a Communist spy. No one had mentioned that recently. Someone must have convinced Mac that Russia really was not a Communist country anymore, and that he sounded pretty stupid when he talked about Commie spies.

I looked again at the clock. Twenty-five of. I glanced toward the lobby. My father was still there! Some of the guys, Woody and Younyoung, were coming in and going straight to our skate room. I certainly didn't want to have to walk past my father picking up trash when kids on my team were there. He was probably picking up some dirty, dripping tissue from one of the snot-nosed little kids. Disgusting! But, I didn't want to be late for practice, either. I usually liked about twenty or twenty five minutes to get ready. I did things slowly, making sure that every piece of equipment was put on just right. If I really had to, I could get ready in less than fifteen minutes. I would be cutting it close soon.

At ten of, my father would ring the bell and open the door to get the Zamboni on the ice. He usually filled it with water first. And so, at any second, he had to be heading out.

I looked back to the rink. They were still going up and down the ice, on the whistle. It was still boring. I expected that if you got really good at figure skating, it would be fun. Trying to make the Olympics would be exciting, kind of like with us, trying to make the Montreal Cup tournament.

The Montreal Cup. I had been thinking about that a lot recently. After tying our first game, we had won three games in a row. Hartford was the easiest. The next game, against Lawrence, hadn't been too hard. That was the game I was suspended for. I wasn't even allowed on the bench! I had started watching it in the stands with my father, but all he did was criticize our team, so I finally moved off by myself to the corner, and watched from there. Lawrence was small and we pretty much dominated, but they did have a couple of very fast forwards. They stole the puck and broke out for about five breakaways that game. They scored on two of them, and we won 4-2, but the game was not as close as it sounds from the score. The North Shore Eagles, a fourth place team the year before, had been our toughest opponent. We went to their rink in Lynn for the game. Mac played amazing hockey, and we won it 1-0. I had a few great hits, the coaches said. In our last game, I scored a goal, and we won 5-3. It was against the Junior Crimson, which was a big and dirty team. It was the first game where the other guys had more penalties than we did! Our power play was crackling that day. We scored three times with a man advantage. My goal was a power play goal, and we had so many man advantages, that all three lines had a chance to play with a man up.

Our record was now 4-0-1, and we had a shot at Montreal. We were playing the two top teams in the league over the next two weeks. If we could win both, it would put us in great shape to make the tourney. We'd be tied for first. If we won just one, we'd still have a shot, but it would be pretty tough.

Lost in my thoughts, I suddenly realized that it was getting late. I grabbed my bag and sticks and raced toward the skate room. My father was still in the lobby, cleaning up a soda that some kid had spilled. I wanted to ignore him, but couldn't. I glanced at him and nodded. He nodded back, but said nothing. Did he know how embarrassed I was about him mopping a floor? I hoped not. I loved my father, and I would not want to hurt him.

Billy came running into the lobby with his bag banging against the doorway. He looked my way and glanced to my father, and then he smirked at me. I wanted to kill him! His father was probably an insurance salesman who couldn't even skate, and my father had played for the Red Army team, but he sees my father cleaning a floor and thinks that I'm a loser because of it. Billy and Mac hadn't been so bad lately. I think that they still hated me, but they had gotten quieter about it with us winning and all. Winning makes everyone happier.

I followed Billy into the skate room.

"It's Mr. Jets and The Enforcer!" Eddie cried out.

Eddie had nicknames for everyone, and they changed all the time. He had been calling me The Enforcer ever since we played the Junior Crimson and I had blindsided their biggest player, Roy LaBomba. LaBomba was the biggest and toughest kid in the league, and he had crushed Little Murph, and so I had gotten even with him. It had only cost me two minutes in the box. If I had done the same thing to a little kid, I might have been kicked out, but smaller kids can do almost anything to bigger kids and not get calls, or at least get less serious ones. Also, luckily, it had been near the end of the game, and so LaBomba never had a chance to retaliate. I was hoping that he would forget by the time we played next.

I sat down on the bench just to the right of Ben.

"Hey, Stas," Ben said.

"Hi, Ben."

"Running a little late, huh?"

"I'll be ready on time," I said, a little defensively.

"I thought that you had to be here an hour early, for Katya?"

"I did. I was watching their practice."

"Wow," Sully said. "It must have been a pretty good practice to keep you this late. All those short skirts and tights, huh?"

"On six year-olds? Like I really care, right," I said.

"I was talking about the Bay State instructors," Sully said, and grinned.

"Oh, man," Eddie said, "now that's one good reason to run late. That tall one with the dark hair and the very short skirt, she can take my mind off hockey!"

I had never even noticed the instructors. I hardly noticed girls at all, and they certainly could not take my mind off hockey.

"I like the short blonde, myself," Bake said. "She's a babe."

"Eh-hem," Moose said, and nodded to Lizzy, who had her head down, tying her skates.

"Don't worry about me," Lizzy said. "I kind of like that tall skinny instructor, the guy with the tight black pants."

"You can have him," Bake said. "Me, I'll take a short blonde any day."

"She's tiny, though!" Drew said. "If you marry her, your kids will be lucky to be five-nine, and you might as well say goodbye to Division One and the NHL."

"My mother is six feet tall," Eddie said. "My dad said marrying a tall woman was the smartest thing he ever did in his life. My doctor says I should grow to be six-three or six-four. Thank you Mom and Dad. NHL, here I come."

"The NHL is great," Woody said, "but the Montreal Cup is a little closer. We have a huge game on Saturday, the biggest of the season. Let's think about that."

Yes, I thought. And I wanted to win it so badly.

Chapter 15

"Stas, can you help me install Sim-House on the computer?" Katya asked.

I groaned. It seemed that all I ever did was install computer programs for Yuriy and Katya over the past week.

"I guess," I sighed. "Get up."

Katya got out of the chair and I sat down at the living room desk, and put the CD into the computer. It was a pain to be the only one in the family who knew how to install software, but at least we had a computer, and we even had an internet connection! Ben's family had gotten a new PC, and Ben knew that we didn't have a computer, so they gave their old one to us. They said that they didn't need it anymore. It was pretty nice, and they probably could have used that one as an extra, but I think they wanted to do something nice for us because we gave Ben so many rides to and from practices. Both his mother and father worked full time jobs and had a hard time getting him to the rink a lot of the time.

Anyway, we actually had a computer, and that was great. And one of my mother's friends, Anna, a lady she knew from Russia who now lived in Boston, well, her husband was a computer genius, and he helped connect our computer to the internet. He did it for free, and it only cost us $4.99 a month for our email and internet. Luckily Anna was a teacher, and she told my mother that kids all need the internet to do their homework these days. My father wasn't wild about the five bucks we had to pay each month. He didn't realize what an incredible deal it was, and he also didn't even know what the internet was. My mother convinced him that it was educational, and so we had a computer with internet. Our connection was slower than a bread line in Moscow, but at least we had it.

Yuriy had spent about forty dollars of his own money and bought a whole box of software from one of his friends, and that's what I had mostly been installing. I sat at the computer, clicking and watching the boxes travel across the screen, which showed how close to done the installation was. Finally, the text window said FINISHED. Yes!

"Can I use the computer now?" I asked Katya.

"But I wanted to play Sim-House!"

"I need to find out something about hockey. It's important! It won't be long."

She shot me an impatient glare.

"Come on, Katya! I've installed about ten programs for you this week! Gimme a break!"

"Okay," she said.

I clicked on the squiggly *I*, which was the internet icon, and waited forever for the phone connection to go through. Finally my home page appeared on the screen. It was my personalized home page, which I had designed with Ben's help, and it was filled with sports links. I clicked on the E-Board. That's an electronic bulletin board for the E Mass hockey league. All the scores and descriptions of games were posted there, as well as any other comments people wanted to make, mostly written by parents and players. It wasn't official, and so you couldn't always believe everything you read, but it was mostly right. People also talked about tournaments, and there were lots of predictions, too. You could write about the kids, but you weren't allowed to use a kid's real name, so you had to use nicknames.

When the E Mass page loaded, I searched for Pee Wee Major in the message category. I looked up, and Katya was standing next to me, arms folded and jaw clenched. I was glad that she wasn't so good at reading. I really did not need to find out anything important. I just wanted to see the predictions for the weekend games. I loved reading different people's predictions.

I spotted 'Pee Wee Major predictions- CB.' CB stood for Crystal Ball. That's what some guy called himself. Ben told me that he was the best at predicting E Mass games. Maybe he really did have a crystal ball!

"Stas," my mother called out from the kitchen, "we're eating soon. You need to set the table."

Darn! It was my turn to do that!

"Katya," I asked, "can you set for me today?"

She opened her eyes widely in protest.

"Please, Katya! I've loaded a ton of programs for you this week! Do me a favor."

She shrugged her shoulders, and said, "Okay."

"Thanks! You're the best sister!"

She smiled politely to me, and strutted into the kitchen to help my mother. Meanwhile, I turned back to the computer, and clicked on Crystal Ball's message. His lengthy predictions filled the screen. I clicked down, searching for his prediction of the Sharks game. It was there, two screens down. I eagerly read.

FW 10 SSS 1

What? The Framingham Wings were going to beat us, 10-1? That guy must be cracked! Yeah, the crystal ball must be cracked, I thought. I read further to see what he thought.

> The Wings are flying to Mont Royal, and no one can stop them. The only ? is what other team with travel N on their tail. The Sharks think it will be them, after 3 straight Ws. But 2 weak opps and 1 great goaltending job by The Truck won't take the Sharks to the Cup. Goon

play can only take them so far. This week, the
Sharks find out they're just little fish in the big
sea.

I cursed at the screen.

"Stas!" my mother said. "Your language! And in the house!"

"Sorry, Mama," I said.

"What are you doing?" Yuriy asked, running over to look at the computer.

"Stas, we get you a computer, and you swear at it like it is person?" my mother said. "Ay-yi-yi. That is not good. That computer, it is for education. And I do not like the education you are giving your sister and brother."

"Damn! Holy ... smokes!" Yuriy blurted out. "They really think that you'll get whipped this weekend!"

"*We come to America, my sons talk like Americans,*" my father said in Russian from his chair. "*Maybe it was a mistake.*"

"Mama," Yuriy said, "maybe he can't talk it, but he sure can understand English. And Papa," Yuriy added, looking to his father, "they swear in Russia, too."

"*Not in my family,*" my father said. "*My father, he would have given me the belt if I spoke as you boys do.*"

"That was the olden days, when Russia was a Communist country," Yuriy said. "It's different now in Russia."

"*Some change is not good,*" my father said.

"Nikolay, you forget what life was like under Communists," my mother said. "It was terrible. People say the wrong thing and disappear. They send you to Siberia then. You did not know who to trust. Even your kids could turn you in, and they be heros in the Young Pioneers. It was a terrible life."

"*But the bread lines were shorter,*" my father said.

"There are no bread lines here," my mother said. "And there is freedom."

"*Freedom to disrespect,*" my father said in Russian.

"I can't understand Papa," Katya said. "What's he saying?" She paused, then continued, "My life is really bad. I can't play hockey. I have to do stupid figure skating lessons in Hingham. I can't play on our new computer because my brother is making me set the table instead. And I can't understand anything Papa says!"

"You don't want to understand him," my mother said. "He is talking nonsense. He lives in this country, but his heart, it is still in Russia. Not the real Russia, though. A Russia that no longer is there. One that never really was there. He remembers only some of life then." She paused. "*Selective memory,*" she added in Russian.

"Papa, you should read this," Yuriy said at the computer. "The guy who wrote this about the Sharks sounds just like you! It says that the Sharks aren't very good, and that they're just goons."

"Humph," my father said, and continued in broken English. "That computer must be smart really. And to think that I thought it was all *brikhnya*." *Brikhnya* means nonsense.

"It's not the computer, Papa," Yuriy said. "It's the internet."

"Then internet must be smart. Who is internet?"

"It's not a person!" I laughed.

"What is internet?" he asked, still in English.

"Information," Yuriy said, "from everywhere in the world! They have stuff about all the E Mass teams. They have standings from my league. There are newspaper articles from zillions of countries. If you want to know about something, you just go to a search engine, and type in a word or words, and it finds information about it. Like, here, I'll go to GooFind and type in Braintree Youth Hockey."

Yuriy leaned over next to me, and clicked SEARCH and then typed in Braintree Youth Hockey. The BYH home page slowly unraveled on the screen.

"See, Papa? I can click to get team rosters, schedules, game results. It's cool! And look, it knows about almost anything. What do you want to know about?"

My father just grunted.

"Come on, Papa. What do you want to find out about?"

"Try the Red Army team," I said. "I bet he'd like to know the latest on them. His newspapers are a week old."

Yuriy typed 'Red Army hockey team' into the 'Search' box, and clicked.

Crisscrossing black hockey sticks on a red background slowly materialized on the computer screen. Photos and statistics filled the lower half of the web page. It was the Red Army hockey club's home page!

"Look, Papa," Yuriy said. "You want to see how they did last night?"

Yuriy clicked.

"You can look at the results yourself," Yuriy said. "Come here!"

My father didn't move.

"Yuriy," my mother said. "You know that your father cannot read English."

"But it's in Russian! Papa, come see!"

My father's head popped out of the newspaper he was reading. Eyebrows raised, he pushed himself out of his chair and walked to Yuriy and me at the computer. I got out of the chair.

"Sit here, Papa," I said.

My father sat down and intently read the Russian description of the game. At least that was what I thought he was reading. I could only read Russian a little.

"How do I get to next page?" my father asked.

I clicked on the scroll-down bar, and he read some more.

"And those words in blue," I said, "if you click on them, you can find out more about those things. Try."

My father looked at me, puzzled. I took his hand and put it on the mouse, and moved it to a link. His large, strong hand did not look right on the tiny computer mouse. And touching his hand felt funny to me. I used to love to hold his hand when I was young. When my little hand was held firmly by his big strong one, the world felt right. Sitting there at the computer, I couldn't remember the last time I had touched his hand. Feeling a little sad and a little happy, I directed his finger to the left button of the mouse.

"Press right here," I said.

He did so, and the hockey page disappeared, and slowly the screen was filled with a beautiful woman in slinky clothing holding what looked like a small white un-inflated balloon.

"What is this!" my father yelled. "Get it off of here! Where did the hockey go?"

I directed my father's hand to the BACK link, and pushed his finger down on the button of the mouse. The Red Army page returned. I wondered what it was in the box that the woman had been holding. Whatever it was, it seemed to get my father mad and embarrassed. I wondered if it was a condom ad. We had learned about AIDS in school, and they showed us what condoms were. I was pretty sure that's what the lady had been holding. No wonder my father had gotten mad. He was pretty old fashioned. We did not talk about sex in our house.

His eyes opened wide as he read on.

"*Next page?*" he asked in Russian.

I clicked the 'page down' bar. He read some more, then reached for the mouse himself, and clicked to the next page.

I glanced at my brother and smiled.

Chapter 16

I gaped at the Wings as they stepped on the ice. They were huge! They all looked like Bantams! I turned my attention back to my own team. We were skating in circles on our half of the rink, loosening up for the big game.

After a minute, Mac hopped into the goal, and the skaters formed two lines in the corners. I was in the front of my line, and began to skate. I rounded the outer face-off dot and skated toward our goal. Sully slid me a perfect pass, and I wound up and fired a slap shot, which Mac easily caught in his glove and tossed aside. I skated to the rear of the other line.

My eyes traveled back to the other end of the rink, where the Wings were having three guys break out of their zone with a complicated weave pass routine, then they turned around and made two other passes before one of their giant guys fired a hard wrist shot at their net. Their goalie moved with confidence and stopped the puck. This was going to be a very tough game.

Moments later, the horn sounded, and we all skated toward our bench. As soon as we had gathered together, Coach Murphy spoke.

"This is it, boys. We have had three good weeks. We have proven that the Sharks can play hockey and win at the Triple-A level. But can we be the best of the best? Are we good enough for Montreal? That's what we're going to find out over the next hour. I'll tell you this, we cannot win this game unless we get the better of them physically. They are a very skilled team. We need to punish them."

I glanced at the Wings across the ice, huddled around their coach. They looked even bigger standing together than they did skating. Punishing them would not be easy, but if that was what we needed to do, then I would do my part. The Wings stood between us and Montreal, and I wanted to play in that tournament more than anything in my life.

"Listen," our coach continued, "everyone has to hit, not just Eddie and Stas. They have set the tone all season. They will need to play even tougher, and all the rest of you will need to follow their example. I'm told that this is a very physical team. It's going to be a war out there. Is anyone afraid to fight it?"

No one said a word.

"Is anyone?" he asked again.

"No, coach!" Eddie cried. "Let's beat 'em!"

"Yeah!" all the kids screamed.

"Win, win win!" Eddie shouted, with the rest of the guys joining in.

"Win! Win! Win!"

The horn sounded, and we quieted down.

I skated to the center red line along with Ben and Lizzy. Eddie and Moose were starting on defense. I lined up at my spot on right wing, and looked up at my opposing wingman. He must have been almost six feet tall! He was taller than my father! He was probably slow, though. Most big guys were.

The Shark parents were screaming encouragement to us. The Wing parents seemed quieter. They had won the league the year before, and so this was probably just another game to them. But we needed to prove something. I needed to prove something. I wanted to show that stupid Crystal Ball that he wasn't so smart. When we won, I could write on the E-Board something like, "Hey, CB, I guess the Sharks have teeth after all." Now, that would be fun!

The ref released the puck, and Ben won the face-off. He dropped the puck back to Moose, who flipped it into the offensive zone. I forechecked hard, but the Wings defense quickly controlled the puck. I charged the puck-handler, who slid a pass to his partner at the last second. Two quick passes later, and the Wings had it at center ice. I sprinted hard to backcheck. The Wings had a three-on-two. Their center controlled the puck and broke to his left, sliding a perfect pass to their left wing, who was cutting back to the middle. The guy one-timed a slap shot. It was a rocket! Mac kicked his right leg pad out, and made a great stop. The Wings right wing was there and drilled the rebound at our diving goalie. Luckily, it went into Mac's chest. He cradled the puck against his body with both arms, and leaned over to protect it. The Wings center was hacking away at Mac as the whistle sounded. A second later, Eddie barreled into the kid, cross-checking him in the back. The guy was big, but he went down hard. The ref blew the whistle as the big Framingham Wings forward slowly pushed himself up off the ice.

"That's a cross-check," the ref said to Eddie. "And after the whistle. We're not going to stand for that."

"I was just protecting my goalie!" Eddie said.

"Not after the whistle, you don't. You won't do him much good in the box."

I skated toward the bench via the penalty box, giving Eddie five as he stepped into the sin bin. As I took my place on our bench, Coach Murphy was all over me.

"Stas, what happened? You didn't touch them!"

I had sprinted as hard as I could. They were fast! I couldn't get to them, but I had tried.

"You were dogging it out there! Or were you afraid? You're awfully tough against the little guys. Against some guys your own size, where is it?"

I said nothing. I wasn't afraid. I wanted to hit someone, but I couldn't. Did he want me to just skate up to some random guy out of the play and flatten him? I'd be in the box for sure.

"Come on, defense!" Coach Murphy yelled to our players on the ice. "Box! Box!"

The box is a defensive position for when the other team has a power play. Your four players form a tight square, letting the other team pass all they want from point to point, or into the corners. The defense's job is to make sure the other guys don't pass into the middle to get a close-in shot. I know about the box from watching hockey on TV. The Sharks had never practiced the box, but somehow, Coach Murphy expected us to know it.

Woody and Drew were back while we had Little Murph and Sully skating forward. Billy was sitting. Poor Billy would lose a lot of ice time because Coach Murphy would never sit his own kid when we were short-handed, and Sully was a better defensive player than Billy. Of course, I didn't mind, because Billy was kind of a jerk, but it still did stink. I knew how mad I'd be if it were me sitting so much.

The Wings moved the puck around the offensive zone like professionals. Twice they set up decent shots from the point, but Mac stopped them both. Finally their left wing slid into the center of our box, while their other wing slid him a pass from behind the net. The guy instantly fired a hard, low wrist shot. Mac was sliding over to cover, but the puck found the five-hole between his split pads, and went in the net. We were down 1-0.

At full strength, Bake, Younyoung and Will got a few of shots on goal the next shift, but none were very hard, and there were no rebounds. And then the Wings broke out of their zone with an amazing pass up the middle, and their center had a semi-breakaway. With Moose right on the kid's tail, the guy couldn't go left or right, and Mac charged him and took away his angle completely, smothering the shot. The whistle blew.

"You know what to do, Stas," Coach Murphy said to me as I skated out to begin my second shift of the game.

They controlled the puck from the start, taking it into our zone, and passing it perfectly whenever one of our guys got near them. I counted the guys we had on the ice. Me and four others. It felt like we were short-handed!

Thirty seconds into the shift, I hadn't even hit one guy. My shift would be over at any second. I would surely get an earful from my coach. A pass went to their defenseman on the left point, the guy I was supposed to cover. He set up to fire a slap shot. I charged hard at him. He faked the shot and pulled the puck aside as I went flying by the guy, skating completely out of the zone. Uncovered, he took three steps toward our goal, wound up, and fired. He unleashed an incredible slap shot that whistled past Mac's ear and hit the twine in the upper left corner of the net. The Wings had scored again! They were up 2-0.

I knew that I wasn't supposed to charge like that. It's too easy to fake a guy if he does that. But I also knew that if I didn't hit someone, Coach Murphy would yell at me.

Slowly, I skated back to the bench. Coach Murphy was seething but didn't say a word. He wouldn't even look at me! On the ice, the Framingham Wings continued to dominate. It seemed that no matter what we did, it wasn't enough. The Wings were too fast and too strong. The final score was 8-0.

I remembered how long Coach Murphy yelled at us after our first tie. It would be a long time before we would see our parents after this game.

Chapter 17

I didn't want to, but I had to. I clicked on the E-Board. I wondered if anyone had commented on our game. I clicked on Pee Wee Major Scores.

> FW 8 SSS 0
>
> No surprises in this one. Wings proved once again that they were the best. Sharks did not belong on the same ice. Hard to believe that Sharks have won as many as they have. All E Mass teams are good, but clearly there are two tiers in this league.

I felt sick. And then anger began to well up inside of me. I wanted to write a response saying that whoever wrote that comment must be a Wing parent, but deep down, I knew that what the person said was true. We didn't belong on the same ice with the Framingham Wings.

Coach Murphy was wrong. He yelled at us after the game saying that we didn't skate hard enough or play physical enough. That wasn't true! We all killed ourselves out there. But it wasn't enough. I wasn't sure if they had better players, or were better coached, but whatever it was, we didn't come close to winning. It was depressing. One more loss, and we would be out of Montreal.

"Is right," my father said to me in English.

I jumped. I didn't know that my father had even left his chair, yet there he was, looking over my shoulder. I also didn't know that he could read a word of English. He had quit the English class my mother had signed him up for after the first week.

"You know," he said, "that writer know your team."

"My team? We just had a bad game! Everyone has bad games!"

"You guys didn't pass the puck," Katya said from the couch. "How can you win without passing?"

"What do you know?" I said angrily. "You don't even play hockey! You just figure skate, if you can even call it that!"

"She knows hockey," Yuriy said. "She plays more street hockey than you do! When you're practicing in the afternoons, she's usually playing in Brendan's driveway. And when you play against me and Katya, and we beat you, it's because we pass the puck, not that we're better than you. Your Triple-A Sharks don't even pass the puck as well as my Squirt team, which hasn't lost a game yet! You were right about those little Mites who came up. They are good. But everyone on your team just stick-handles, or dumps the puck or shoots."

"We made some passes," I said.

"A few," Yuriy said. "The Asian kid, Number 11, he made a lot of nice passes, and the girl, too, but they were about the only ones. Will, he didn't make one pass the entire game! And Billy keeps his head down, so he has no idea where any of you other guys are."

I wanted to argue, but I couldn't. Yuriy was right. I used to pass the puck pretty well, but Coach Murphy just talked about hitting, so that's mostly what I did. That and shoot, but I didn't get any chances against the Wings. Younyoung Lee did make some nice passes. He was probably the best passer on the team. Funny, he was the one Coach Murphy yelled at the most. Younyoung wasn't much of a hitter.

"You out of the Cup?" my father asked.

How did he know about the Montreal Cup? I thought that he never listened to any stuff like that.

"No," I said. "If we win the rest, we should be in."

"Cup, shmuck," my mother chimed in from the kitchen, as my father returned to his chair. "I work all day in the house, and have outside job at the supermarket, all so you can play hockey in the E Mass league, and this is what I get. Why do it? I should keep you on the Braintree team. That is just as good. Your team was terrible today. You were terrible."

My father? My sister? My brother? Even my mother? It was too much to take! I wanted to scream. The game was bad enough. Coach Murphy was bad enough. But now I had to listen to my whole family tell me how bad I was and how lousy the team was. I was torn between lashing out and arguing, and crying because they were right. I almost wanted to quit hockey. Almost. But I still loved the game, even when it was terrible. I couldn't imagine life without lacing up my skates and getting on the ice.

I looked down to see the other scores. The good teams pretty much killed the lousy teams. There were some close games when two evenly matched teams played.

Maybe that E-Board person was right. Maybe there were two levels of teams, and we were in the lower level. That was probably why the league had second division playoffs. In E Mass hockey, the first six teams played in league playoffs at the end of the season. The seventh through tenth place teams had another set of playoffs, for a battle to be the best of the second best. This year, the Pee Wee Major year, nobody much talked about the playoffs. Everyone was thinking about ending out in the top two after the first thirteen games, when each team had played each other once. Everyone was thinking about the Montreal Cup. Well, at least the good teams were, and the Sharks thought of themselves as a good team.

I skimmed the comments about the various other teams. You could tell who wrote each comment, or at least whether it was a kid from the winning team or the losing team. Kids or parents from the losing team usually complained about the referees. Parents from the team that won usually called it "a well played game by both sides." It's easy to be a good sport when you win.

One of the Huskies broke a collarbone. That kid would be gone for a while. I felt bad for him, but mostly thought, "Thank God that wasn't me." I had never missed more than one game in a row from an injury. I prayed I never would. The pain I could live with, but missing hockey games would be worse than being exiled to a gulag in Siberia. That's a prison you got sent to if you weren't a good Communist. Every time I read about a kid who got injured, I remembered the guy I had hurt earlier in the season. He had broken his leg. At least they didn't talk about him anymore on the E-Board.

I scanned the titles of the other messages. I didn't care about scores from other divisions, but sometimes they talked about things like the Montreal Cup or college scouts. Just then, though, there was nothing I wanted to read. Weekend messages were mostly scores and game comments.

"Mama, can I use the computer?" Katya asked.

"Why don't you ask your brother?" she called in from the kitchen. Something smelled pretty good in there.

"He always says no," Yuriy said, "and she'll end out asking you anyway. She might as well not waste everyone's time by asking Stas in the first place. He thinks he owns the computer."

"Ay-yi-yi," my mother said. "Do I look like a referee?"

"*They cannot settle disputes without a referee,*" my father said in Russian, but continued in English. "My sons, they never once play hockey game without referee. In house, Tati, you are the referee. In Russia when I was boy, every neighborhood has outdoor rink where kids play and there be no adults. We play, we fight, but we do it ourself. American kids need referees and coaches or there be no game."

"You don't need to referee us," I said.

"Right, Stas," Yuriy said. "And you'll sit at the computer the whole time because you're bigger than us."

"Right," Katya said.

"I'll be right off," I said. "I just have one more thing to check."

I exited the E-Board and clicked on my email. There were three messages, two from Ben and one from Younyoung. I clicked on Ben's first message.

> Stas, I'm bummin about the game. Do you think that we can still make the Montr Cup? We need to win the next 8 games, right? Those wings were good! 68

Ben always signed his emails with '68.' That was his number on the team. I clicked on his second email.

> Stas, can you come to my house for the night after next Saturday's game? If you can, bring your roller blades and the movie Slap Shot. I like the hockey fight movie if you want to bring that. I just got the newest NHL Live video game. It's awesome! These two guys were shirting each other when the ref tried to break them up and he got slugged. You'll love it. Hey, did you hear about the guy who took his family to see a boxing match, when a hockey game broke out? My father told me that. 68

The NHL game sounded cool!

"Mama, can I go to Ben's after the game on Saturday?"

"If you stay out of trouble," she answered from the kitchen.

"Mama, what smells so good?" I asked.

"Onions."

"Yuch!" I said.

"You should try them," she said. "Fried onions, they so sweet, they are almost like candy."

They did smell good. Maybe I should try them, I thought.

"What's for dinner?" Yuriy asked.

"Liver and onion," my mother answered.

"Aha!" my father said with glee. "A real meal!"

"Gross!" Katya said.

"I hate liver!" I said.

"Me too," Yuriy said. "Why can't we have cold cuts like we usually do?

"You don't like this? Then you no eat it," my father said.

I would eat it, though. Choke it down was more like it. I knew that liver was loaded with protein and would make me a lot stronger. Each bite would add muscle and bulk. I'd imagine getting an extra goal for each mouthful. Yeah, I'd get through it.

I was finally ready to check the email from Younyoung Lee. It had taken me a ways into the Shark season before I realized that Younyoung went to my school. He had gone to a different elementary school, and our middle school was so big that I didn't know most of the kids. Plus, Younyoung was so quiet that no one noticed him at school, and all those Asian kids had always looked alike to me anyway. They all hung out together, and some of them didn't even talk in English when they had lunch in the caf. Younyoung was not in any of my regular classes, but it turned out he was in my gym class, along with about forty other boys. One day, we had a floor hockey tournament, and he was on my team. The first shift, he deked his way down the whole gym floor and slid me a perfect pass on a 2-on-0 for a score. Without even seeing his face, I knew that it was Younyoung. I could tell by the way he moved and passed.

The next day, I sat down next to him at lunch, and we didn't say a word, but he smiled at me when I joined him. Some other Asian kids sat at that table, and they spoke half in English and half in a foreign language, which I later found out was Korean.

I didn't have any other real friends at school, so I started sitting with Younyoung every day, and one day, he actually started talking to me. His friends all called him Lee, not Younyoung or Youn, so I started to call him Lee too. It seemed dumb since one of the other kids he hung out with was also called Lee, but they all knew who was talking about who.

Lee told me that he was Korean. I used to think he was Chinese. He said that there was a big difference between Korean and Chinese. I also found out that he hated to be called Youn, because 'young' was his generational name, and was even more important to him than 'Youn.' Being a generational name meant that all the boys in his family had 'young' as part of their name. His one brother was named Moonyoung, which meant 'great scholar.' Younyoung meant 'person of great success.' Lee was a really cool kid, and smart, and probably would be a success someday. His friends were pretty nice, too. And they had cool names, like Jin-Soon, Tong-Lin, Junseong and Chul. And they always shared their Korean desserts with me. I knew when Kim's grandmother had visited because he brought in *song-pyun*, which were really sweet rice cakes, shaped like half moons.

I still hung out with Jimmy Duval a little, but he never shared his dessert with me. He wasn't mad at me any more for leaving the town hockey team, but I didn't think he liked me either. I really didn't like him and wouldn't have spent any time with him at all, but if the only kids I ever sat with were the Korean kids, people might think that I didn't have any other friends, and that I was a loser.

I clicked on Lee's email. As I began to read, I could see his smiling face. I found it hard to believe that I used to think that Lee and his Korean friends all looked alike. Now that I knew them, they looked as different as any group of Russian or American kids. My eyes went back to the top and started reading again.

> Hi Stas. Tough game. You played good, tho. One of my friends just called me and said that he heard that Jimmy Duval was going to beat you up at school on Monday when you play mug freeze. Jin-Soon is pretty tough. Do you want him and me to hang around your bus pickup after school? That's when you play mug freeze, right? Lee

Geez! I didn't want to get in a fight. Not with Jimmy Duval. I wasn't afraid of him, but if I beat him up, it would just start a big thing with him and his friends. But it wouldn't help to have Lee and his friends get involved. I instantly clicked RESPOND.

> Lee, Thanks for the warning. I can handle Duval myself. We don't need to start a race war. Those idiots think that all the Asians are the same. See you at school. Stas

Those idiots, I thought, almost laughing at myself. I used to be one of those idiots. I was glad to have a friend like Younyoung Lee at school.

I signed off my email, and turned to Katya and said, "All yours."

"Finally!" she huffed.

Chapter 18

That Monday was a funny day at school. Jimmy sat next to me on the bus and was the friendliest he had ever been. I was glad that Lee had warned me about him. Otherwise I would have been psyched that he was treating me so nicely, and it would have really crushed me when he sucker-punched me after school. During the day, all of Jimmy's friends, mostly kids on the town hockey team, seemed especially nice to me. They must all be in on this, I thought. And with too many people knowing something, you can't keep a secret. Someone told someone they shouldn't have, and that person must have told Lee.

I really did not want to deal with the fight thing that day. The terrible loss to the Wings was more important, and I needed to come to grips with that. I needed to figure out some way to get my team to turn it around and win. We'd get killed by the Terriers that coming Saturday if we didn't do something different. But I wasn't able to think about hockey very much. I needed to decide what to do about Jimmy.

Mug-freeze was a game that Jimmy and his friends played a lot while they were waiting for the bus. I used to play it with those guys all the time in 5th Grade recess. The teachers made it illegal, but we found places to play it anyway. There was no recess in the middle school, but the kids sometimes still played the game after school.

Mug-freeze was actually a pretty cool game. One kid was 'it' and counted out, "1,2,3,4,5,6,7,8,9,10, mug freeze!" At that second, everyone had to be completely still, frozen like a stop action picture on TV. If anyone moved, the kid who was 'it' might say, "Billy moved!" Then Billy had to call out, "1,2,3,4,5,6,7,8,9,10, mug freeze," while people pounded him until he was done counting. Then everyone stopped again, usually frozen in mid-punch form. It was cool when a fist was frozen an inch away from a kid's face.

The kid who was 'it' tried to get someone to move by throwing a fake punch and stopping just short of hitting the guy. He hoped the kid would flinch or something. But if the guy who was 'it' accidentally touched one of the frozen kids, the kid who was touched would say, "He touched me!" Everyone then beat on the kid who was 'it' while he counted to ten again and called out, "Mug freeze."

I was one of the best at this game. No one ever made me move. I wasn't afraid of anyone. If a kid accidentally hit me, I would have pounded him to a pulp, and the kids all knew this, so they never came too close to me with their fake punches. Sometimes I would move on purpose just so I could be 'it.'

Now, this probably sounds like a pretty brutal game, but it really wasn't too bad. You played this with friends, and no one hit very hard or punched you in the face. Mostly, you punched in the arms and chest and back, and only hard enough to hurt a little. But if someone wanted to really hurt a kid in mug-freeze, it would be easy to do. All day I wondered what Jimmy had in mind. Would he try to be 'it', and just walk up to me and smash me in the face? That would hurt. Or would he slip a few hard punches in when everyone was hitting me when I was 'it'? That way, I might not know who it was that nailed me, but he couldn't get me quite as good. I would have to be ready for both.

The day seemed to take forever. Even math class, which was usually my favorite, was endless. In Ancient History, we learned about the Trojan Horse. That was pretty cool, and that was the only class that didn't drag. Two armies were fighting in ancient Greece, and one group just couldn't get past the walls of Troy, the city they were attacking. Finally, the attackers just disappeared one morning. They left a huge wooden horse. The people of Troy thought that the attackers had given up and left the horse as a gift to the brave defenders of the city. They rolled the horse past their gate and into the city, and had a huge victory party that night. The morning after the party when all the people of Troy were sleeping, soldiers from the attacking army who had been hiding in the horse snuck out and killed everyone. Mr. Dow told us that that was where the expression "Beware Greeks bearing gifts" came from.

To me, it said that the element of surprise was critical in a fight. Surprise the other guy, and you win. How could we surprise the Terriers this Saturday? How could I surprise Jimmy Duval after school? I felt like those Greeks attacking Troy. I knew something that Jimmy didn't know. I knew what Jimmy had in mind, and he didn't know that I knew it. What would I do? How could I take advantage of that?

At lunch I sat with Lee and his friends. Actually, they were my friends, too, but I still thought of them as Lee's friends.

"Are you okay for after school?" Jin-Soon asked in a heavy Korean accent.

"Yeah," I said. I wasn't afraid of Jimmy Duval.

Jin-Soon nodded, and continued eating. I liked that about those guys. They weren't all in your face about stuff.

I forked a piece of hot dog and paused. I wasn't really hungry, but I might need the energy after school. I forced myself to eat it. It was from breakfast. I was glad that Lee's friends didn't make fun of me for bringing in breakfast leftovers for lunch. I did that a lot because it saved money, money that could be spent on hockey. A school lunch was three bucks, the same as a skate sharpening, and I liked my skates razor sharp. I continued to work my way through my plate of cut up hot dog. Jimmy and his friends always laughed at me when I brought my own lunch to school. It was usually leftover meat from breakfast, and they always said that my family was weird for eating hot dogs for breakfast. I told them that most people in Russia had hot dogs for breakfast, but they only laughed at me some more.

Jin-Soon, Tong-Lin, Junseong and Chul mostly talked Korean for the rest of the meal. I didn't mind. I wasn't paying any attention to what they were saying. My mind was elsewhere. Lee was pretty quiet himself. I think that he was nervous about me getting hurt.

In the afternoon, science class was deadly. It was a lecture on atoms, and there's nothing more boring than atoms. They're so small you can't even see them! And so you can't do experiments, which is the best part of science class. What were we going to do, build an atomic bomb?

Luckily, my last class of the day was art. We were all making heraldic designs, which was a design that might be put on a knight's shield or flag. I was making mine completely from hockey sticks, crisscrossing each other at different angles. I'm usually not very good at art, but this picture was starting to look pretty good!

At last the school bell rang. It was 2:45! Lost in my art project, I had forgotten about Jimmy Duval for a while. Now, I'd have to deal with that. I still wasn't sure what I would do, but I would be ready for him.

I went to my locker, packed up the books I needed for homework, and left the rest. Just as I was closing my locker, Jimmy came up behind me and said, "Let's go! We're having a quick game of mug-freeze before the bus comes."

I nodded and followed Jimmy toward the door. I passed the main office, and glanced in. Mr. Dedekian was looking up and waved to me. He worked at one of the computers outside the principal's office. He did data processing. Mr. Dedekian was the only person at school besides me who spoke Russian. He had moved to the United States from St. Petersberg about ten years ago. I think he liked me because I was the only Russian kid in the school. He liked to talk in Russian to me. I waved back to Mr. Dedekian, and followed Jimmy out.

We went straight to the parking lot alley where the rest of the guys were hanging out.

"Let's start," Jimmy said. "Who wants to be first?"

"I will," Corky said. Corky's name was really Jack Corcoran.

"One, two, three..." he began.

We all lightly pounded on him.

"...four, five, six, seven, eight, nine, ten, mug freeze!"

I intentionally moved a second after the count. It thought it was better to be 'it'. I made sure I was a distance away from the pack.

"Stas moved!"

"One, two, three, four, five, six, seven, eight, nine, ten, mug freeze!" I called.

No one had even gotten to me until I got to nine, and Jimmy had been completely boxed out. That's how I had planned it. I took one or two light blows to the back, and that was it. Everyone was frozen. Jimmy was just behind Jack. Jack was frozen in classic mid-punch form, like a stop action shot just before a Mike Tyson blow. Jimmy's hands were both clenched tightly into fists, but hung down by his sides. I approached Jack and did a circular left-to-right punch in front of his face. My fist came so close to his face that I would have grazed a hanging bugger with my knuckles. But I didn't touch him. Thank goodness he didn't have a runny nose. I was the best at coming close to a kid without touching him. I stepped past Jack and got to Jimmy. Maybe I should just flatten him now, before he got a chance at me. He'd be shocked! But that wouldn't be right. I'd wait for him to make a move, and I would be prepared to defend.

I did a fake punch to Jimmy's stomach, not coming close at all, when he suddenly drove his fist into my stomach.

"Stas moved!" he called out.

"No I didn't!" I said, coughing in pain.

All the guys began to beat on me, hitting me hard in the arms and stomach. I fought back, but one against six was pretty tough. Finally, I called out, "One, two, three, four, five, six, seven, eight, nine, ten, mug freeze!"

The boys all stopped in their tracks.

My stomach killed! I felt like I wanted to throw up. That had not been the usual light hitting. I was so mad at Jimmy, and at all the other kids. I stared at them and they smiled back at me. My blood began to boil. I might be able to nail one of them now, but the others would kill me. I hadn't been prepared for Jimmy to do what he did. I thought being 'it' had made me safe.

I stepped up to Jimmy, and pulled my arm back from his face. I could send him to the hospital now, I thought. Those guys had been smart. They had all hit me where there wouldn't be any marks. Maybe I wanted to leave a mark. I was so mad that I didn't care about anything except hurting these kids. But I wasn't stupid.

"Look out!" someone behind me cried. I turned around instantly and saw Charlie Galvin's fist coming right at my nose. I ducked just in time, as Charlie's punch cut though the empty air, landing in Jimmy's surprised face.

"Ow!" Jimmy yelled. "What'd you do that for?"

"Sorry!" Charlie said. "Get him!"

I turned to run, but someone grabbed my leg and I fell forward on the hard pavement. Charlie was leading the other guys to me, while Jack held my foot. I tried to yank it away, when Lee flew into the alley and kicked Jack hard in the stomach. Jack let go of my leg and jumped up. Jimmy was almost on me, and I pulled back my right fist and punched him square in the face. Ow! My hand killed! It looked a lot easier in those hockey fights on TV.

Jimmy dropped to the ground, screaming. Lee punched Richie Clougherty in his huge stomach, and Richie collapsed into a pile of jelly, whimpering. Jimmy was still screaming, with his hands over his face. Bright red blood was dripping down his chin.

The other boys stopped dead in their tracks. It was like real life mug-freeze.

"Help me!" Jimmy yelled. He was crying like a little boy.

"Stop!" a voice boomed.

We all froze. It was Mr. Eaton, the assistant principal!

Mr. Eaton ran over to look at Jimmy.

"Move your hand!" he said to Jimmy.

Jimmy took his hand away from his face. His nose was a mess of blood.

"Jack, run to my office and have them call an ambulance. The rest of you boys, go right to my office and wait there for me!"

Jack took off quickly while Richie, Charlie, Lee, me and Jimmy's three other friends sheepishly followed.

Chapter 19

The parents had been in there forever. Sitting outside Mr. Eaton's office, time seemed to have come to a standstill. What could they be talking about for so long? At least my father had been working, and it was my mother who came to school to talk with our assistant principal. And it was lucky that Mr. Dorsey, the principal, was out of town. He was much more strict than Mr. Eaton, who kind of had a 'boys will be boys' attitude about things. I didn't actually know that myself. I had never been in trouble before. But Jimmy Duval talked a lot about Mr. Eaton, and really liked him, even if he made Jimmy do tons of detentions.

"I'm in huge trouble," Lee whispered nervously.

"We all are," I whispered back. Jimmy's friends were all squeezed on the bench opposite us. There wasn't room on the bench for five, but none of them wanted to sit with Lee and me, and they were practically on each other's laps. Jimmy was in the hospital, and so he was the only kid in the fight who didn't have a parent talking to Mr. Eaton.

"No, you don't know my parents," Lee said in a hushed voice. "This will cause my parents to lose face, and there is nothing worse to them."

Losing face means to be embarrassed or ashamed. Younyoung Lee sometimes used funny expressions like that. Even though he was born in this country, his parents came here from Korea as adults. They had learned the English language from classes, like we might learn French or Spanish in school. They must have learned from a book published in the 50's or earlier, because they used a lot of expressions that you only hear old people use, and Lee learned to talk that way from them.

Poor Lee looked terrified. He was chewing at his fingernails like a vulture pecking away at road kill.

"Lee," I said, "you're going to get in the least trouble of anyone. You were the only one who wasn't playing mug freeze! Didn't you hear Mr. Eaton go on and on about how that game was the cause of all the trouble? Everyone admitted what happened, mostly, except that those guys lied about one thing. They said that I started it by punching Jimmy in the nose, but it was Galvin who hit him."

"Yeah," Lee said, "but I don't think that Mr. Eaton believed them."

"Well, if he knows that you weren't playing mug-freeze, you're okay."

"Then why did he call my parents in? My mother and father are always talking about keeping my nose clean."

That's another one of those expressions he used, and it means staying out of trouble.

Lee continued in a whisper. "There are the Vietnamese kids who hang out in a gang and are always in trouble. Even worse, there's a group of Korean kids from Quincy who are nothing but bad news. My parents speak of those kids' parents like they are dirt. My mother and father believe that a child's behavior is a reflection on the parent. To be called in to the principal's office is a terrible thing. It will bring shame upon my whole family, both here and in Korea."

My parents were pretty strict, but Mr. and Mrs. Lee sounded much worse. Still, I couldn't believe that people in Korea would be gossiping about this. I might get seriously punished, but there was no way that my relatives in Russia would know about it. And if they did, it wouldn't be that big a deal.

I looked across at Jimmy's buddies. They looked bored and a little impatient, but not scared. I think a lot of them had spent some serious time on Mr. Eaton's bench.

The door to Mr. Eaton's office suddenly opened. A bunch of
mothers and two fathers walked out as a group, followed by my
mother. At the end, Mr. and Mrs. Lee solemnly stepped through
the doorway.

I wasn't sure whether we were all going to go in again, or just
leave. Or maybe Mr. Eaton would want to talk with us
individually. At the beginning, Mr. Eaton had said that he'd hear
from us all, then speak with the parents, and he'd decide what
would happen next.

My mother did not crack a smile as she walked up to me.

"Is that it?" I asked.

She nodded.

Mr. and Mrs. Lee were already escorting Younyoung out of
the building. He turned around and nodded to me. Good luck, I
thought. My friend would need it.

I followed my mother to the car. She did not way a word, and
neither did I. I slid into the back seat as she took her place in
the driver's seat. We buckled our seatbelts, then she started the
car and began to drive home. I was waiting for her to say
something, but she didn't. When I couldn't stand the silence any
more, I spoke.

"Well, Mama?"

"Well, what?"

"What did Mr. Eaton say? Did he say what the punishment
would be?"

"You have five days of detention."

"That's all?" I asked. I thought for sure I'd be suspended,
with Jimmy in the hospital and all.

"He told us that playing that foolish game mug-freeze was the
real offense. He didn't think that anyone planned to fight, but
that it just happened. That game is too rough and makes people
want to fight."

"Actually, Jimmy and his friends did plan to beat me up. That's why Younyoung Lee was there." I always called him Younyoung or Younyoung Lee to my mother, not Lee. She thinks that it's disrespectful to speak of a person just using their last name.

"Why did you not say that to Mr. Eaton?" my mother asked. There was a trace of anger in her voice.

"Right, Mama. Then those guys would really have it out for me. You never rat on other kids."

"Rat?"

"Yeah, rat," I said. "That means to tell adults, like tattling."

"But this boy Jimmy, he is enemy, no?"

"Sort of, but he'd be a much bigger enemy if I ratted on him."

"Honor between thieves," she said.

"So, Mama, did everyone get the same punishment?"

"Everyone except Younyoung. He has detention for just one day."

"Really?" I asked. That was great! Maybe he wouldn't get as wrecked by his parents! "Why?"

"Principal know that Younyoung was not in the mug freeze game. They understand that he was watching and that he only joined in because the other boys were all fighting against you. I don't think that he wanted to punish Younyoung at all. Mr. Eaton almost told Mr. and Mrs. Lee not to punish Younyoung."

"So why did he give him a detention at all?" I asked.

"The other parents, they would have hollered. They were enough upset that their boys got longer detentions than Younyoung."

"Don't they know that their boys are thugs?"

"Mothers never know. Fathers sometimes do, but never mothers. To them, their sons are always the sweet boys that they gave birth to."

"Mama, I'm sorry that you had to come to get me at the principal's office."

"Ugh, yah," she responded. "I believe you that you did not start that fight, but you got in it anyway. I worry about you. Your father, he worry even more. He sees you on this ice, and shakes his head, and says, *galavarez.* How do you say it in English? Head chopper?"

"Actually, in hockey, it's headhunter. But that's a guy who slashes kids in the head with his stick, and I don't do that."

"I don't know. Your father, he call you *galavarez,* and *hooligan.* And now this."

"The ice is different, Mama! My coach, he tells me to hit. The kids on the team, they are starting to like me because I hit. Even Mac is okay to me. I'm sorry about this fight, but I have to do what I do on the ice."

"Your father does not think so."

"Doesn't Papa say that I should do what my coach says?"

My mother started to say something, but stopped.

"Doesn't he?" I asked again.

"I don't know," she said, as she turned into an open parking spot in front of our home.

I prayed that my father was still working. I didn't want him to hear about my day in school. I hopped out of the car and ran to the house. I needed to call Ben and tell him everything that had happened.

Chapter 20

I needed to get my mind into the game. The past week, with the fight and the detentions, I had been pretty distracted. But here I was, ready to begin a do-or-die game against the powerful Tyngsboro Terriers. If we lost the game, we were eliminated from making the Montreal Cup.

My line would be out second. Sully's line was out first. Will's line would be third, but Peter Donohue, our alternate, was playing instead of Lee. I still couldn't believe that Lee's parents were making him take a week off from hockey as a punishment for the fight! He was missing a game, and a huge one! Lee was the best player on that line. Peter wasn't even close to him. Losing Lee might be the difference between going to Montreal or not. Did Mr. and Mrs. Lee realize that they were punishing our whole team by grounding their son for a whole week, even from hockey? I had never heard of any E Mass parents who had punished their kid by making them miss a game.

The E-Board had had tons of comments on it over the week. I don't know how people found out. All the Shark parents knew. Someone must have said something and word got out. Probably Coach Murphy. He had gone ballistic. That's funny, since he was always yelling at Lee to be tougher, you'd think he'd be happy to have him gone.

Anyway, there must have been about twenty parents who wrote about it. Most parents said that it's about time some families had their priorities straight, that hockey is about growing up and learning, and not about just winning and losing. Lots of other parents responded in agreement. They couldn't mention Lee by name, but they called him Shark Passer. Did that mean that they thought he was the only one on the team who passed? A couple parents thought that Lee's parents should have found a punishment that punished only him, and not our whole team. Other parents pretty much trashed those folks, asking them to look at what they had become. I almost understood what those grownups were talking about, the ones that thought Mr. and Mrs. Lee were doing the right thing. But another part of me knew that our road to Montreal had just gotten a lot steeper because of the loss of Lee. And I wanted to go to Montreal. I also felt bad for Lee himself. He was so upset about not playing, and felt that he had let the whole team down.

As the ref was ready to drop the puck, I prayed that Crystal Ball was wrong. He had predicted that without the Shark Passer, the Shark sea would be even bloodier than it had been against the Wings. He had predicted that the Terriers would win 12-1.

The puck was dropped. We controlled it. Eddie dumped it into the zone and Billy flew into the corner to beat the Terrier defense. With two red jerseys barreling toward him, Billy blindly flipped the puck toward the slot. Sully was there and one-timed a slap shot at the Terrier goalie. Sully caught the puck just right, and it took off like a rocket. Sully was incredibly strong. The Terrier goalie did not even see the puck as it found its way under his glove arm and into the net. We were ahead, 1-0! Sully's linemates almost smothered him! We had scored in our first shift against the second place Terriers! Maybe the Terriers were thinking that this would be an easy game, and they were not up for it. Maybe they had spent too much time reading the E-Board and their mind was already on the following week's game. But we were ahead! Suddenly, the road to Montreal was a little less steep.

I went out there with Ben and Lizzy. Drew and Woody moved out on defense. We played the Terriers pretty evenly. Mac, "the

Truck" as they call him on the E-Board, made one excellent save, but their goalie stopped a pretty good bid by Lizzy.

Then our third line went out. From the start, it was a disaster. Without Lee's passing, we couldn't break it out of the zone. Will tried to skate it out every time, and he was always stopped by two or three Terriers. The Terriers stopped covering other guys and just stuck with Will whenever he had the puck. Peter was useless. It was obvious why he was the alternate. I felt bad for him. He loved hockey more than anyone I knew, but he just did not have the talent to play at this level.

The Terriers kept the puck in our zone for about two minutes. Coach Murphy liked to change lines every forty seconds or so, but he couldn't change up when the puck was in our zone. Mac was playing out of his skull, but the Terrier shots were all low, and he couldn't glove any and tie up the puck for a line change. Finally, one of the huge Terrier defensemen fired a wicked slap shot right on the ice. Their center tipped it up and over the outstretched leg pad of Mac and into the net. The Terriers had tied it up.

After that, it was a different game. The Terriers were all over us. Crystal Ball was right, it was a blood bath. The more we fell behind, the more Coach Murphy told us to make them pay. I was getting so mad, that I would have been trying to kill them anyway without my coach telling me to. By the time I was out there for the last shift of the game, we were behind 13-1. And it wasn't Mac's fault. He had actually played pretty well! After two periods, we were down 6-1 and it was obvious that we wouldn't win. The coaches put Tyler in just to give him some ice time, and he got destroyed. He didn't stop much, giving up seven goals in one period. Part of it was that we had pretty much given up, and part of it was our coach. Coach Murphy was going ballistic because the Terriers were piling up the score. He had even yelled at the Terrier Coach about that halfway through the third period. That had cost us a penalty and another goal. I heard the Terrier coach yell to us that as long as we played cheap, he'd ratchet up the goal count.

As usual, on my last shift, it looked like the Terriers had a power play, even though they didn't. Half the game they had been on actual power plays. I had been in the box three times, Eddie three times, Little Murph twice, Will twice, and a bunch of the other kids once. We had had thirteen penalties, compared to just three on the Terriers. Those refs in Tyngsboro were terrible. They were obviously on the side of the Terriers. I saw one of the refs laughing with the Terrier coach between periods, like they were friends.

The Terrier defensemen took one shot after another from the point. Finally, Tyler pounced on the puck, and the whistle blew. A half second later, a Terrier forward was digging at the puck from under Tyler. He got the puck out and slid it in the empty net. The ref waved 'no goal.' Wasn't thirteen goals enough? I was so mad! I sprinted toward the Terrier forward with both hands on my stick, and cross-checked him right in the back. He went down hard. Another Terrier blind-sided me, and I was on the ice. I looked up and saw Eddie Germano punching a Terrier, the guy who had hit me. The guy had his helmet on and Eddie was wearing his gloves, so no one was getting hurt. Still, it was crazy to see Eddie pounding away at the kid like a guy on my World Boxing Championship video game. Eddie took another swing, a huge one, but he slipped and fell, The other guy, who had just been standing there, jumped on Eddie and started to hit him. I jumped to my feet and skated over and slugged the kid. I was reaching back to hit again when one of the refs dragged me away.

That was pretty much the end of the fight. By the time the refs sorted everything out, Eddie and I were kicked out of the game. Coach Murphy was kicked out, too. I guess he had been swearing at the ref after he found out Eddie and I were gone while one Terrier kid just got two minutes for roughing. I didn't even know it then, but the kids later told me that Mac's father had been kicked out of the rink. I guess he wouldn't stop yelling at the refs and he almost got in a fight with one of the Terrier parents. There was only about a minute to play, and so getting kicked out didn't matter, but it did mean we would have to miss the next game.

At that point, as I skated off the ice with Eddie, I didn't even care whether or not I played the next game. We weren't going to Montreal, so what did it matter? If only Lee had been here, I thought. Then again, the way they had killed us, it probably wouldn't have mattered. I didn't want to talk to anyone on the team, not even Ben. I just wanted to go home.

Chapter 21

The night after that game, I just waited to get yelled at by my father. He hadn't said a word to me on the ride home. It had just been him and me. My mother was with Yuriy at his game, and Katya had gone to Yuriy's game because they were in first place, and we were lousy, she said. Lousy! We were an E Mass hockey club! If she wanted to see lousy, she should have looked at all the kids at her stupid learn-to-skate figure skating lessons!

Anyway, that night at the table, no one said anything about me or the Sharks. They just talked about Yuriy's game, and how great it was.

"It was awesome," Katya said to my father and me. "We were down by two goals in the last period and came back and won! Yuriy scored three goals!"

"Your first hat-trick, yes?" my father asked in English. More and more he spoke English in our home. I think it was because Katya didn't understand much Russian.

"He's gotten tons," I said. He had. It was no big deal.

"Yeah, in rec league," Yuriy said. "but that was nothing."

In our first year in Braintree, both Yuriy and I had played in the town's rec league. That's because my parents did not know that travel hockey started in September. At the end of the fall, after soccer season had ended, my parents had looked to sign us up for hockey, but the only league that started then was the winter rec league which ran December through February. I was a Squirt and Yuriy was a Mite. We both looked like Wayne Gretzkys out there. People even got mad at us for playing in that league, saying we belonged on a travel team and were ruining things. Anyway, we both went straight from there to travel A teams the next year. That's like going right from Juniors to the NHL.

My father's face lit up, hearing about Yuriy's game. All I could think, as I ate my beef goulash, was that he was wishing that he had been to Yuriy's game instead of mine. They always split up when we both played at the same time. I wondered how they decided who went where. For the next game, they might draw sticks, and the short stick would be stuck with my game. A month earlier, I had thought the opposite. I felt bad for the parent who got stuck with a town Squirt game when they could be seeing Triple-A Pee Wees.

Finally, my mother said, "So, you got in another fight?"

"Another fight?" I asked. "This was my first fight! This was the first time I've ever been kicked out of a game for fighting!"

Suddenly, my mother tightened up. She looked embarrassed, and said nothing.

"She's talking about your fight in school," Katya said.

"Katya!" Yuriy said.

"Fight in school?" my father said. "What fight?"

"Woops!" Katya said, putting her hand over her mouth.

They hadn't told him about my fight in school? I couldn't believe it! I thought that parents told each other everything! Why hadn't my mother told my father? No wonder Papa had not yelled at me for that. Yuriy, Katya and my mother all looked back and forth to one another. I felt out of it. It was like they had this conspiracy, and I was not part of it. I was an outsider, like our alternate Peter Donohue on the Skarks, and I did not like it.

"*Tell me about the fight!*" Papa demanded in Russian.

My mother breathed in deeply, and slowly released the air from her lungs. "Okay," she said. "It was a small thing, and I did not want to worry you. It was a play fight, a game, and someone accidentally hit someone else, and soon, there is real fight."

"Why no one tell me?" my father asked.

Nobody said a word.

"Well?" he demanded.

I finally spoke. "I'm sure that they didn't want you to get mad like you do after every one of my Shark games. I can't wait until I play for my school team, and we get to go home from games on the team bus."

"How dare you talk to your father that way!" Mama cried.

"My family," my father said, "what goes wrong? In America, children do not respect adults. Too much America. In Russia, sons not grow up to be *hooligans*. In America, my son is *galavarez*."

"We used to fight in Russia, too," I said. America was my country, and I hated it when he said bad things about it. And we did fight back in Russia. My father would always threaten to send us to Siberia if we did not behave. "And there were gangs in Moscow, too."

"You, with your behavior, you embarrass me," he said quietly. "I am glad to be in America where my family and friends cannot see you."

"Embarrass!" I said. "Do you know what it's like to have your father spend his day cleaning up people's candy wrappers off the floor of the skate room?"

My father glared at me. "I not hungry," he almost whispered, as he got up from the dinner table. He left and headed to his bedroom. I gulped. My father never went to his bedroom, except to sleep. He always retreated to his big armchair, but I could see his faded green chair from the kitchen table, and it sat there empty. I felt terrible.

"Stas!" my mother said, almost hissing. "How dare you! Your father, he works very hard so you have a good home. He leave all he loves to come to this country, and all for you and Yuriy and Katya. He wants a better life for you."

"I'm sorry," I said.

"Sorry is not enough," she said. "Your papa, he takes great pride in his work. There is no one who takes more pride in making good ice than your papa. He does more than clean floors. He fixes the Zamboni, fixes the heater in rink, keeps the ice pipes working. Your team has the best rink because of your father. But if all he did was sweep floors, and he did it well, he can be proud."

I felt sick. Why had I said what I said? My mother was right.

"I'm not hungry," I said quietly. "Can I leave?"

My mother nodded.

I got up and walked down the hall to my bedroom, and shut the door behind me. I lay down on my bed, and the tears suddenly came to my eyes. I tried to hold them back but I couldn't. In seconds, I was crying like a baby. I was crying about what I had said to my father. I was crying because of my terrible season. I was crying about everything. This was going to be such a great year, being with the Sharks and all. What had gone wrong?

The phone sounded, and after four rings, my mother answered. I strained to listen to her.

"I'm sorry, he can't come to the phone now," my mother said.

After a brief pause, she said, "I'll tell him. Bye."

It must have been for me. My father almost never got phone calls, and when he did, the caller usually spoke Russian. But my mother had talked in English. I wondered who it had been? Either Ben or Lee. Probably Ben, since he called me the most, but it might have been Lee, since he hadn't been at the game that day.

I didn't want to talk with anyone, but part of me was bursting to talk, to get it all out of my system. It had been a good week in school after the fight. Detention was no big deal. I just sat and did my homework, something I always do in the afternoon, because I usually had hockey at night. Jimmy Duval was not mad. He acted as if nothing had happened. He actually seemed friendlier than usual. I think that he was glad that I hadn't told Mr. Eaton about who started the fight. I had been getting really psyched about the Terrier game. But then in one afternoon, my world fell apart. The Sharks lost and were out of Montreal, we were playing pretty lousy, and my father thought that I was a terrible person, a *galavarez*. And after what I had said to my father, I thought I was a terrible person. That's even worse than having someone else think you're bad.

Chapter 22

The next week was a rough one. At home, my father barely spoke to me. He pretty much grumbled to everyone in the family. In hockey, I knew that I wouldn't get to play against the Bedford Bruins on Saturday, and that was the only game for the weekend. The next three weeks, we had two games each weekend. Why couldn't we have two games this weekend so I could play in one? Having no games at all to look forward to was torturous. It made practice almost seem like a chore. My heart wasn't in it like before. It didn't help that Coach Murphy just wanted to kill us every second we were on the ice. And reading the E-Board was painful, yet I couldn't stay away. Everyone ripped into the Sharks for playing like goons and for being lousy. In school, Lee was pretty cool toward me. I kept asking him if he was mad at me, and he said no, but Jin-Soon told me that his parents did not want him to be good friends with me. They heard about the fight at the game, and said that I was a bad influence. Lee was my only good friend in school and one of my two best friends on the Sharks! He was such a good kid! It crushed me when Jin-Soon said that about Lee and his parents.

Everything was going bad, and there didn't seem to be anything that I could do about it. Would it ever get better, I wondered? Or would this be my life from now on?

That Saturday, I went with Ben to the Shark's game while both of my parents went to Yuriy's game. I didn't blame them. I wasn't going to play, plus it was a long drive to Bedford. Driving to a game and not playing is torture that you can't believe. The only good part was that Eddie wasn't playing either. We sat together in the stands, and Eddie was so funny, that by the time the game started, he had me laughing and laughing.

He was imitating the coaches and all the parents, and he had them down pat. He did a perfect Coach Murphy, yelling at everyone to hit harder, and he did a great take-off of Mr. Mackay, Mac's father, swearing at the refs and at the parents of the other team. Eddie pretended he was Mr. Sullivan, who was so intense that he tuned out everyone around him and just talked to himself the whole game. He did a hilarious Mr. McKenzie, criticizing all of Will's linemates for not passing the puck to Will, which is pretty funny, since Will never passed the puck to anyone! Mr. MacKenzie also talked nonstop about how his kid was on the "right track" to the NHL. Next, Eddie mimicked Mr. Bacon analyzing the game like a college professor, which he was. He taught physics at MIT. After that, Eddie impersonated Billy's father, who was always cracking jokes and talking about women. He said he was writing a book called *Hockey Moms in Negligees*. I had to ask Eddie what negligees were. Eddie said they were sexy nightgowns. I tried to imagine my mother in a negligee. I couldn't. She still wore the thick flannel night clothes which had kept her warm in our drafty apartment through those cold Moscow winters. Eddie's best imitation was of his own father, who did nothing but yell, "Hit him! Play the body!"

I asked Eddie how he knew so much about the parents. He said that he had been kicked out of a bunch of games last year, and sat with the parents. He described it as a real education. It's funny, we all make fun of Eddie for being kind of stupid, but I don't think that I would have noticed all those things about the adults. I guess that you can be smart in different ways.

I tried to concentrate on the game, but it was actually pretty boring. Eddie was more fun to listen to.

On the ice, Coach Murphy was going with two centers and three sets of wings, and playing three 'D'. He didn't call up Peter to play this game. As alternate, Coach Murphy had told the

Donohues that Peter would play if we were short anyone, which does happen a lot, with injuries and occasional family commitments. But after the game against the Terriers, Coach Murphy did not want Peter to play with us, even if Eddie and I were sitting. He thought that the team had a better chance with a short bench, and so he had told Peter that he was appealing the suspension, and that Eddie and I would play at Bedford. It didn't feel right to have a coach lie, but we did have a better chance to win without Peter. He was just too slow. I still felt bad for the kid. If he ever found out what Coach had done, he'd be devastated. He loved hockey as much as anyone I knew.

The Bedford Bruins were a below .500 team, and we should have beaten them easily, but the Sharks came out flat. We played the game just as we had skated in practice the week before, without heart. Going into the third period, we held a slim one goal lead, on top 3-2. And then, from the start of the third period, the Bruins were beating us to the puck everywhere. Our centers and defense were playing short, and it looked like they had lost their legs. Bedford quickly tied it up on a breakaway goal where their kid made a great deke on Mac. The next shift, Bedford went ahead on a deflection off of Moose's skate. The Sharks seemed to give up then, and the final score was Bedford Bruins 7, South Shore Sharks 3.

I was pretty depressed about the game, but Eddie just shrugged it off, cracking more jokes. I wished that I could be more like Eddie, and just laugh off problems. But I wasn't funny and popular like Eddie, with a million friends. I had two friends, but lately it was more like one.

I looked across the rink and saw the parents getting up and heading for the warm concession room and their post-game coffees. I noticed Mr. and Mrs. Lee rise from their usual spots on the bleachers. They were seated a little outside the cluster of Shark parents. I wanted to go up to them and tell them that I wasn't a bad kid, and that I was a good friend of Younyoung's. Of course, I didn't have the courage to say a word to them. When I had gone over to Lee's house before, both his mother and father seemed so serious and reserved that they made me nervous. Now, they hated me and didn't want Younyoung to be my friend. Younyoung's family was very important to him, and I knew that he would obey them.

"Come on, let's get a hot chocolate," Eddie said. Because we were suspended, we were not even allowed to be in the skate room after the game. At least we wouldn't have to listen to Coach Murphy yell at us. That was the only good thing about not playing.

"Okay," I said. Eddie lived on Cape Cod, which was an hour away from Braintree. I wished that Eddie lived closer. It would be fun to have him as a friend.

Eddie barreled his way through the lobby, and I followed. In moments, we were somehow at the front to the line. It wasn't really a line, though. A swarm of people just formed in front of the concession window, and everyone moved forward slowly, except Eddie, who slipped through the crowd like a hot knife through lard. Lard is like butter, and was used instead of butter in Russia.

"One hot chocolate," Eddie said, shivering. He turned to me, and said, "Man, I'd rather be playing. It's cold as a witch's butt in those stands!"

I didn't know that a witch's butt was cold, but Eddie made it sound funny when he said it.

"Yeah," Eddie said, "the jewels headed north sitting on that cold seat." He smirked.

I wasn't exactly sure what he meant by that, but I think the jewels were supposed to be 'the family jewels.' I knew what those were. Kids talked about those on the streets of Moscow. I laughed.

"Aren't you having a hot choc?" Eddie asked me.

I didn't have any money.

"Nah," I said. "I'm not that cold." I tried to stop the chattering of my teeth.

"No cash, huh?" Eddie said. "I'll treat."

Eddie called out to the young teenage girl behind the counter, "Make that two hot chocolates!"

The skinny blonde girl nodded and turned back to the hot chocolate machine. She wore a dirty white apron over a sweater and short skirt.

"She'll be something in a couple years, huh?" Eddie said.

"Yeah," I said, without really even looking. I wasn't as interested in girls as Eddie, but if I were, I'd be more interested in athletic girls, like Lizzy.

The blonde girl came over and handed us two steaming hot chocolates.

Eddie paid, and dropped the change into a Styrofoam cup that had TIPS written on the side. She smiled.

"Investing in the future," Eddie whispered to me, and winked.

"Thanks," I said, taking my hot chocolate.

A minute later, we found ourselves walking through the Shark parent gathering.

"We could have used you guys out there," Mr. Sullivan said.

"That's for sure," Billy's father said, almost looking over my shoulders as he spoke. Was he checking out the hockey moms, I wondered? Gross! Mothers aren't like girls. They're just mothers.

I took a sip of my drink. The hot chocolate tasted great! It almost burned my throat, but it warmed my whole body.

"Eddie, my man," Mr. Germano said to his son. "You did a hell of a job out there. You robbed the Bruins of five or six powerplays!"

"Thanks, Dad," Eddie said.

"What is he talking about?" I whispered to Eddie.

"He thinks I spend too much time in the box, and so by not playing, the Bruins didn't have as many power plays. But he also thinks I should hit more. I can't figure him out."

But at least he was there, I thought. Eddie didn't play, but his father came to the game anyway. Not my father.

Fifteen minutes later, the Sharks emerged from the team room, dragging hockey bags, sticks, and long expressions. Ben walked straight up to me.

"One period!" he said. "If we could only get back one period! We were killing them in the first two periods, but we died in the third."

Mr. and Mrs. Shelley, Ben's parents, walked up behind me as Ben spoke.

"It's just like the Boston Bruin's announcers always say, you have to play sixty minutes of hockey out there. Forty ain't enough."

"Thirty-six in our case," Ben added, " and it ain't enough to put in twenty, uh, .."

"Twenty four," I added. I was better at math than Ben.

The Bruins were the only team in the league besides the Sharks which still played twelve minute periods. Cheap owners, a lot of the parents said on the E-Board. Fifteen minute periods were much more fun to play. But watching this game, I was glad they were playing twelves.

"Do you want to come over my house?" Ben asked.

I thought for a second.

"Naw," I said. I was too miserable, and didn't want to feel any better. I deserved to feel bad. If I went to Ben's house, he might make me forget how sad I was. "I think I'll just go straight home, if that's okay, Mr. Shelley."

"Of course," Ben's father said. He was supposed to drive me home. "Next week's another week and another game."

I just prayed that it would be a better week and a better game.

Chapter 23

Coach Murphy droned on and on. I hardly heard a word he said anymore. The other kids didn't listen much either. I don't think that Coach Regan even listened, and Coach Regan was his friend! We had lost thirteen of our last fourteen games, with the only non-loss being a second tie to the last place Hartford Devils, the joke of the league. Things had gotten so bad that I had stopped reading the E-Board altogether. We were in thirteenth place out of fourteen teams. We were about to play the Devils for the last time this season. If we couldn't beat them, we'd probably not win another game. We were virtually out of contention for the second tier playoffs.

The only item of interest to any of us was which team we might play on the next year. Nobody wanted to stay with the Sharks, except the kids who weren't good enough to make another team. I was mad because I knew that the fathers of a lot of the other kids were calling coaches and making agreements for the following year. The way E Mass worked was that every kid was like a free agent at the end of each season. No agreement was official until a contract was signed after the last playoff game, but parents and coaches talked all the time. Some parents would tell five different coaches that they wanted their kid to play with that coach's team. Coaches, too, made promises that they didn't keep. It could get pretty ugly. E Mass mating season, they called it.

And my father would have no part of it. My father was so disgusted with the Sharks that he almost never came to my games. My mother came, but only if Yuriy and Katya weren't playing.

Katya was actually playing hockey, and my mother and father both chose to see her games instead of mine. They said that it was because she was so young and it was her first season, but I knew it was because they hated Shark games. As bad as my games were, they were better than Katya's. She was on a Mite C travel team for our town. It turned out that Mr. O'Neil, Lizzy's father, was coaching the Mite C team for Braintree. I didn't even know that Lizzy lived in Braintree, because she went to a private school. Anyway, her father was coaching because she had a brother playing in his first year of Mites, and in the middle of November, there were two openings. That's because the Heafy twins, who were both on the team, had to move because their father got a job in California. Lizzy told her father about Katya, and he had asked Katya if she wanted one of the two spots. Katya begged and begged Mama and Papa to play, and they finally said okay. Katya has a way of breaking down a 'no,' especially Papa's. Also, the O'Neils lived only about a mile from our house, and Mr. O'Neil would be able to drive Katya to practice every day, since we were on their way to the rink.

I tried to focus my attention back on the pregame talk, but as Coach Murphy said the same old stuff about hitting and hustling, my eyes wandered to my teammates. Billy, Little Murph, Eddie, Moose, Drew, Bake, Will, Ben and Woody all looked as spaced out as I felt. Their glazed eyes stared straight ahead while their mouths hung open. Mac and Tyler weren't even looking anywhere near the coach, but then again, goalies are always in their own world. Lee wore an expressionless face, with his eyes fixed on our head coach. He might have been listening to every word Coach Murphy was saying, or his mind might have been elsewhere. Lee always showed that same respectful, attentive face, so it was hard to tell what he was thinking. Sully and Lizzy were the only two who seemed to be really listening to our coach's speech. As I scanned their faces, I was thinking that I was probably the only kid to not have a parent watching this game. I had told my mother that I didn't really care whether she came, but I did care.

Finally, the horn sounded from out in the rink. At last. It wasn't that I was psyched to play, but I couldn't stand one more minute of Coach Murphy's blabbering. I followed Lee out of the locker room. I felt sad that we were no longer friends. I think that he still wanted to be my friend, but his parents had forbidden it. He never actually told me that, but I knew it anyway. I sometimes sat with him for lunch at school, but he didn't talk much to me, so I usually sat with Jimmy and his friends. Sometimes I sat by myself.

My line was starting against the Devils. The lowly Devils, as they were called on the E-Board. Why would you ever name a team the Devils? Where does the Devil live? Way down there, in the basement, so to speak. It seemed only right that the Devils were in the basement of the E Mass Hockey League. There were lots of E-Board comments about the Devils being at the bottom. These Devils, though, seemed fired up to play us. The Sharks didn't seem to care. Even Mac looked as if he had given up. I didn't even have the energy to hit kids, which was about all I did well that season. If the Devils gave us a few cheap shots, I might get inspired to hit. I hoped so.

The ref dropped the puck and Hartford controlled it. Our guys all seemed to be going at half speed, while the Devils were flying. They had gotten a lot better since the last time we had seen them! They buzzed around Mac and did everything but score. Finally, Mac tied up the puck and we got a line change. Coach Murphy was yelling at us on the bench. I think that he was embarrassed by our team. I know that I was.

With Billy's line out on the ice, we did no better, and the Devils finally scored in a scramble in front of our net. By the end of the first period, we were down 3-0. Coach Murphy talked about pride in his thirty seconds between periods, but we had nothing to be proud of, not the way we played hockey. Lizzy was the only one out there hustling for us. She always came off the ice gasping for breath and looking like she was ready to throw up.

My little sister Katya had been right all along. We never passed the puck. We also didn't play our positions very well. Hitting can get you only so far in hockey.

At the start of the second period, one of their big guys creamed Billy. Sure, we all know Billy goes down every game, but this was worse. Usually, he lay still for a minute, got up, and was skating his next shift, but this time, the coaches had to carry him off the ice. One of their guys had given him a leg check. The refs gave the kid a five minute major.

"You gotta be kidding me!" the Devil coach yelled.

"That's enough, coach," one of the refs said, the tall one with a pock marked face and one tooth missing. The other ref was a teenager.

"You're enough," the coach said.

"That'll cost your team a player for two minutes," the tall, tough looking ref growled. "Bench minor."

Billy was not one of my favorite teammates, but he was a Shark, and that Devil had no right to leg check him. I wanted to get even, but Eddie beat me to it. He crushed one of their guys the next shift, while we had a 5-on-3 advantage, but it was a clean hit, and nothing was called. Eddie should have gone for the puck, but he went for the kid instead. The Devil coach screamed at the refs some more.

"Shut your mouth, coach. Not another word. Last warning!"

It was fun to see the other coach in trouble for a change. His name was Dave Curtin, and I had read a lot about him in the E-Board. It was usually Coach Murphy the refs got all over, and lots had been written about him. Coach Murphy had gotten five bench minors this season, and had been kicked out of two games.

"Kick me out, ref, but for the record, I want to protest your officiating. Someone's going to get hurt, and you will be to blame."

"That's enough," the tall ref said. "This is hockey. It's a rough sport. You know what 'not another word' means. Call it a day, coach."

"Gladly," Coach Curtin of the Devils said, and he stepped off the bench and shuffled across the ice. Cheers and hoots rang out from the Shark parent section, while the Devil parents were booing the ref.

"Coach," the tall ref said to an assistant Devil coach, "you need to send someone else to the box. You're still down by two guys. The third penalty will start at the completion of the first bench minor. Number 60 stays in the box the whole time for a major."

The Devil penalty box was packed with three players in there. Ours was empty. It was an unusual sight.

For the first time in a long time, we skated hard. Ben made a beautiful pass to me from the corner into the high slot and I fired. Their goalie stopped it with his leg pad, but Lizzy was on the doorstep and banged in the rebound.

Because they had three men out, we still had a two man advantage. Sully's line went out next, and seemed as inspired as our line had been. Will skated instead of Billy on the wing, and he scored a beautiful wrap-around goal. Our bench was making a lot of noise. So were the Shark parents. Within only a minute, we had cut two goals off the lead. It was now 3-2.

We would have a power play for the next four minutes, no matter how many goals we scored. Suddenly, it was the Devils who looked beat. Sharks got to every loose puck first, and the next time our line was out again, I scored on a low wrist shot to the stick side. The game was tied, 3-3!

Even after the Devils had all their men out of the box and were at full strength, we dominated. We got another goal in the second period, and a fifth goal in the third. That's when the Devils started playing dirty hockey. They began slashing us and throwing high elbows and cross-checking us. The refs were hardly calling anything. Coach Murphy started to get mad and told us that we had to defend ourselves. With two minutes to play, Moose nailed one of their forwards, who had to be carried off the ice. The last two minutes were ugly, but luckily no one else got hurt, no thanks to the refs.

Coach Murphy was so angry at the Devils and at the refs, that he told us not to line up for the post-game handshake. We just skated off the ice. Coach Regan and Coach Murphy were at the end of the line as we exited.

"Awesome game," I said to Ben.

"Finally," Ben said.

"Good game," Lee said to me in his soft voice.

I *had* played well. I had scored a goal, gotten two assists, and was only in the penalty box once! That was a record for me. Yet I had hit hard, too. I don't know if I hit cleaner or the refs called less. I was happy, though.

Just as I was stepping into our team room, I heard someone yell, "Stop it!" I turned around to see what the commotion was. At the gate of the rink, Coach Murphy and the Devil's Coach were holding each other by their shirt collars. Both were big men, and both were angry and red-faced. The tall, tough-looking ref was next to them, trying his best to pull them apart.

"Fight!" Eddie yelled. Our whole team turned around and began to head back toward the rink and the tussling coaches.

I was drawn to the fight, as I was to any fight, but a panic also took hold of me. It didn't look right seeing two grown men on the verge of a fistfight. It was scary.

"In the skate room!" Coach Regan hollered in a booming voice, a voice that I had never heard out of him before.

We all stopped.

"Turn around, now!"

We all did so. Coach Regan walked us into our team room, and shut the door.

"Sit down," Coach Regan ordered us.

We all obeyed.

"You know, you played a great game out there today. The first great game in more than two months. What's going on out there is not funny or exciting. It is unfortunate."

He spoke with an authority that I had never heard from him. He sounded more like a teacher than a coach.

"I don't know whether Coach Murphy is right or wrong. I didn't see what happened. I do know that Coach Curtin of the Devils was waiting for us at the gate. I don't know what he said or did to provoke what happened. I just know that adults fighting can be very dangerous, and does not belong in youth hockey."

"A guy got killed a couple years ago," Bake said. "It was a fight between two hockey dads."

"We all know about that," Coach Regan said. "Two families will never be the same, and that altercation cast a black mark on our whole sport. Now, please, take off your equipment, join your parents, and leave without an incident. If there is any verbal or physical interaction with anyone on the Devils, I will make sure that you never put on a Shark uniform again."

He said it with such finality that none of us doubted him for a second. We quietly began to take off our equipment. Then the team room door opened. Coach Murphy stepped in. His hair was mussed up and his shirt was torn, but otherwise, he looked fine. I wondered what the other coach looked like.

"Boys," Coach Murphy said. "You guys played a great game. I'm sorry that you're not leaving here with that as the only thing to think about."

"Coach," Eddie asked. "Did you win?"

"There was no winner," Coach Murphy answered. "It shouldn't have happened. Dave Curtin, the Devils coach, got a little carried away. I needed to defend myself. The referee got an accidental elbow in the mouth. I don't expect I will be in practice on Tuesday. I'm sure there'll be a league hearing. Coach Regan will take over while I'm away. Whatever happens, just remember, when push comes to shove, a man has to defend himself. You did that as a team out there. I did it as well."

A knock sounded from our left. The whole team looked over, and then the door opened a crack. The smaller, younger ref stuck his head through. He looked scared stiff.

"Uh, er, Coach, let's go," he said meekly.

"Boys, you showed me something this game. Whether I'm here or not as your coach, keep it up. Believe in yourself."

Coach Murphy started to leave.

"Dad, what about me?" Little Murph asked.

"I'll be in the car," my coach said, and left.

No one said a word.

Chapter 24

"Nikolay, Coach Regan does not know hockey," my mother said as she spooned red sauce on our rice. She was right. Coach Regan was just coaching the team because he was an old friend of Coach Murphy.

"Papa, that's right," Katya said. "He's worse than Murphy! Mr. O'Neil is a better coach, and we're just a town Mite team."

I didn't say anything. I just spread the red sauce evenly over my mound of rice pilaf. I didn't like any white to show on top.

My mother thought that my father should volunteer to coach our Shark team. In two weeks with Coach Regan, we had looked even worse than before. We didn't play any better as a team, and we hit even less, which made us terrible! We had lost the last two games by big scores.

We did need a different coach, but I wasn't sure I wanted it to be my father. I could just see the E-Board: *Zamboni Brez takes over Sharks – that's like the janitor taking over Microsoft!* I knew that my father had played on the Red Army team, but I had never actually seen him play, and I had no idea what kind of coach he'd be. At that time, not everyone knew that the Zamboni guy at Hingham was my father. If he coached the Sharks, everyone in the league would know that I was the kid of Zamboni Brez.

"I will not coach!" my father said.

Whew, I thought.

"Why?" Katya said.

"Yeah, Papa, why?" Yuriy asked. "Every time I do what you tell me in hockey, it works. You see things all the time that my coaches don't. Like picking up a man on defense, always moving and keeping my head up. I'd stink if it weren't for you! You'd be awesome."

My father did know a lot about the game, and he was helpful when he said stuff, as much as I hated to admit it. I did not like to be criticized, but when he told me what I was doing wrong, he was usually right.

"The season be almost done," my father said.

"We still have ten more games to go," I said. It sounded as if I wanted him to coach. Did I? And if he agreed to volunteer, would they let him? What about when he was supposed to work?

"They can still make the second division playoffs," Yuriy said.

"No way," I said. I knew that we needed to win most of those games to have a shot at tenth place. "Not our team. It stinks!"

"No," my father said. "Sharks not stink. Your team, you have talent. You just do not use it."

"That's why you should coach them," my mother said firmly.

My father just grunted.

"Do it, Papa!" Katya said.

I wondered if he would be good? Maybe he would. Sitting there at our kitchen table, part of me wanted him to try it.

"No one would understand me," my father said in his thick Russian accent.

"No one understands Coach Murphy," I said. "He just yells and it echoes in the rink, and you can't understand half of what he says."

"Nikolay, your English is getting much better," my mother said.

I thought about that a second, and realized that it was. Since sometime in the fall, he had begun to speak only English in the house, unless he got mad or was on the phone with a Russian guy. It was probably Katya who got him to do it, since she complained that she didn't understand Russian. Actually, I think that she did understand it pretty well, and that she just said that she didn't. One time, when she said that she didn't know what my father was saying, I saw Katya and my mother smile at each other, like they were sharing a secret or something.

"You should do it," my mother said.

"Yeah, Papa," Katya said.

I looked at my father. Sweat was pouring down his forehead. His eyes seemed filled with fear. My father was afraid! Suddenly, I felt bad for him. I had never felt that way about him before. My father who was always so strong and sure, he was not supposed to be scared. Maybe angry, yes, but not afraid. I did not want to see him like that.

"He does not want to do it," I said. "Leave him alone."

My father gave me a funny look. A little thankful, a little sad. I didn't know what he was thinking. He breathed deeply, and cut into his pork chop, and continued eating. That was the end of the discussion.

After dinner that night, my father sat in his chair and read his Russian newspaper. There was no practice for anyone that night. It was strange, all of us being home. Yuriy and I sat down to do homework at the kitchen table while Katya went to our bedroom to play with her dolls. She liked to play house with them, but the dolls usually ended up playing a game of hockey on the floor, like Yuriy and I did with our plastic hockey action figures. Her dolls were pretty beat up. I don't think they were built for that kind of play.

After a while, my father moved over to the desk and turned on the computer. I still couldn't get used to him at sitting at a computer. It didn't look right. But once he found out about the web sites for all the Russian hockey leagues, and that they were in Russian, he was at the computer every night. He found all sorts of Russian stuff on the internet. He liked that he got information about a week before he'd get it from his Russian newspaper.

He had bought a Russian language CD, which let him type in Russian. He had learned how to use email, and he emailed a few guys that he knew in Moscow.

After I finished my math, I quietly cruised over to the computer to see what he was doing. He was at the E Mass web site, looking at the E-Board!

"Papa! What are you doing?"

My father jumped, and quickly closed the web page.

"Nothing."

"Papa, that was the E-Board. And it was in English! I thought that you couldn't read English?"

My father hemmed and hawed, and turned a little red.

"Were you reading that?" I asked.

"Go do your homework," he said.

Yuriy and my mother were staring in our direction. Open-mouthed, neither said a word. I was sure that my father had been reading the E-Board, and in English! I was stunned. Why did he not admit it? He was funny about English. Always had been. He was so afraid of looking stupid because he couldn't speak or understand English well enough. That was why he didn't want anyone to know about his playing for the Red Army hockey club in Russia. People would want to talk to him, even if he had a hard time with English. Instead, he wanted to be just the Zamboni guy who quietly did his job at the rink.

I obeyed my father and returned to the kitchen table. I turned to my history reading. I read the words, but they did not really stick with me. I kept on thinking about Papa. Did he know English better than he said? How had he learned it? He had quit the class that Mama had signed him up for. Or had he? He had been acting a little mysterious lately. I tried to think how. Actually, there had been a number of times that I came into the house and caught him scurrying away from the computer or saw him shutting down a program. I struggled with my reading, but kept an eye on the computer and on my father.

I saw him closing the internet access program, and I called out across the room, "Papa, don't turn the computer off. I need to look up something for Social Science."

My father nodded. I walked across the room and sat at the computer. The chair was warm. I clicked onto the internet, and went to the 'History' button. That tells you all the web sites that have been visited recently. I saw the NHL site, an E-Mass site, a bunch of Russian sites, the ESPN site, and then saw www.esl.com. What was that? I clicked there.

ESL, the site read. Underneath, it said, 'English as a Second Language.' It was a web site for teaching English as a second language! My father had been learning English on the internet! I read some more. It was cool! You clicked on your native language, and on a level, and it gave lessons! I suddenly recalled coming in one day and seeing him stick something in his pocket as he was walking away from the computer. I thought they were our headphones. That seemed strange, but now I understood. This explained a lot. It explained why he was speaking in English all the time, and why he was so good with the computer. I clicked further back in the History. He had been taking English lessons since November! That was two months ago. He had visited the site almost every morning that we were at school. Unbelievable.

Suddenly, a wave of guilt swept over me. I felt like I was spying on him, kind of like I was rummaging through his bureau drawers. I wanted to tell Yuriy and Katya, even Mama, but it didn't seem right. I didn't know what to do. Instead, I clicked to the E-Board, and checked out Pee Wee major messages. I searched for the Sharks in the subject line. I found one.

New Shark coach may be a nice guy, but hockey has gone from bad to worse. Sharks have hit the depth of the ocean. Can't go much deeper.

I read the response to that.

Yeah, but at least there not a durty as they ust to be.

While I smiled at the spelling, I suddenly decided that I wanted my father to coach the Sharks for the rest of the season. But I couldn't ask him. I saw how much he did not want to do it. I would not be like Katya and ask and ask. If he didn't want to coach, he shouldn't have to coach. But I hoped he would.

I clicked on other Pee Wee messages, about big games coming up that would determine which teams would make which divisional playoffs. The Montreal Cup was over, and the Framingham Wings had been the silver medal winner. That meant that they were the second best Pee Wee team in the world! The Terriers had gone too, and they did a decent job. But it was good to have that over with. Everyone's attention was back on our league, not that any of that mattered for the Sharks. I still checked out the messages, wishing that we were in the hunt for something. Staying out of last place was all we could hope for.

Chapter 25

As soon as I stepped through the entrance to the Hingham Sports Arena, Ben practically pounced on me.

"Stas!"

"What is it?" I asked, surprised and puzzled.

"Stas, I'm sorry. I did something that I shouldn't have done."

"What?"

"I told my father about your father."

"Huh?"

"I told him that your dad played for the Red Army team. We sat down at the computer together, and he checked out all his stats on the internet. It was hard to find a site that had all that in English and not in Russian, but we finally found it. Stas, your father was awesome!"

I didn't know that there was stuff on my father on the internet. I hadn't found it. But then, again, I hadn't looked for it.

"He led the league in scoring one season, and was league MVP. He would have gone to the Olympics, except he broke his wrist that fall."

My mouth dropped.

"And he played in the Montreal Cup when he was our age. His team won it."

My father had won the Montreal Cup? My legs suddenly felt shaky and I walked over to the bench to sit down.

"I'm sorry, Stas," Ben said. "I know that you told me not to tell."

"That's all right. I'm not mad. I just didn't know about all that other stuff."

"You didn't? About your own father?"

"No."

"Geez, if my father was that good, he'd let everyone in the world know. I hear every month about how my father won his college's intramural Scrabble championship. Every time he loses to my mother, he says he got lousy tiles, and tells her about winning that college thing."

"My father isn't like that at all. He doesn't like people to notice him."

"He's shy?"

"Yeah, and I think he's embarrassed about not knowing English too well."

"Well, I'm sorry for telling my Dad," Ben said.

"If it's just him that knows, then that's okay," I said.

"Uh," Ben began awkwardly. "Uh..."

"What?"

"Uh, you're not going to like this," Ben said.

"Just spit it out. We have to get dressed for practice."

"Stas, my father called all the other parents on the team. He thinks that your father should coach the Sharks."

"What?" I yelped.

"Stas, he is disgusted at the coaching we've gotten all season, especially for all the money we pay to be in this league. He thought Murphy was a joke, and he didn't like him. My dad likes Regan as a person, but says that he's a worse coach than Murphy. Leland McSweeny is the owner of the whole Shark franchise, and Mr. Mackay is pushing to be the new coach."

"Mac's father?"

"Yeah," Ben said. "He wants to coach, and is the only parent who played hockey after high school. He was a star at Quincy North, then tried making it as a walk-on at Northeastern. He never made the team. He played for some D3 team for a season, then flunked out of school. He tried to play juniors, I guess, but took too many shots to the head and had to stop playing. But I heard he gave as many as he took."

"And he wants to coach us?"

"Yeah. That's why my father called the other parents, and they're having a meeting during our practice to talk about it. My father wants your father to coach, and it sounds like most of the other parents want that, too. McSweeny will be there."

I didn't even know what Leland McSweeny looked like, but I had read about him on the E-Board. He was in charge of all the Shark teams. He helped get us ice, hired coaches, took care of money, and stuff like that.

"My mother is here at the rink with me. Is she going?"

"No," Ben said. "we didn't call your parents. My dad thought it would be best if the team decided that they wanted your father first, then asked him. Your parents shouldn't be there when some people are arguing whether they want Mac's father to coach. It could get ugly."

I didn't know what to think. My father would kill me! And what would my mother think when all the other parents disappeared? That would be weird. On the other hand, she hardly spoke with any of them, except Ben's mother, and Ben's mother was not even there. His father was at the rink instead. My mother would probably not even notice that all the other parents were gone.

"Stas, let's get dressed for practice."

I followed Ben into the locker room.

"Stas, my man," Eddie said. "Why didn't you tell us that your father was an all-Russia hockey star?"

"That is so cool," Bake said. "My father told me."

"But do you want the guy to coach us?" Mac asked. "My father has seen guys that can skate like the wind, but there're stupid as bricks and couldn't coach their way out of a paper bag."

"My father is not stupid!" I shouted.

"Right," Mac said. "That's why he sweeps floors for a living."

"My father was a mechanic in a factory in Russia," I said. "He was a foreman! He is very smart."

"I guess the other guys can't be very smart in your country, if they made him the boss."

"Hey, Mac, shut up," Billy said. I was shocked. Billy was Mac's best friend on the team.

"Just telling the truth," Mac said.

"My father is on the rink's board," Billy said, "and he said that this whole place would fall to the ground without Zamboni Brez. The Zamboni is about thirty years old, and Stas's father keeps it working. The condenser is even older, and Mr. Brez is always fixing it so we have ice."

"Well, excuse me," Mac said. "Your father is on the board. Well, my father played in the AHL and was almost called up to play for the Kings."

"Some people can skate like the wind, but are stupid as bricks," Woody said. "I don't know about you, but I hope that Zamboni Brez will coach our team. Our parents are all meeting now to talk about that."

"I hope he does, too," Moose said.

"Me, too," Ben said.

"Sure," Mac said, "you're Stas's friend."

"I think that Zamboni Brez should be the coach," Eddie said. "I love freaking Ruskies! Did you ever see the tape of Team Russia against Team Canada back in the 70's? They were a tough, lean, mean, passing machine. They would have beat the Candians easily if Bobby Clarke hadn't broken the ankle of the best Russian player. He went out there and just hacked the guy."

"The Russian player was Valeri Kharlamov," Peter said.

"Whatever, it was awesome," Sully said. "Bobby Clarke is my hero. That was a war back then!"

"Those Russians, they were a team," Eddie said. "I'd like to play like them. Make the other teams have to break my ankles to have a chance at beating us."

"Right now, all they have to do is walk and chew gum to beat us," Tyler said. "That would be a switch. I hope Stas's father gets to coach us."

At that moment, Coach Regan walked into the room.

"Come on, guys, you'll be late!"

"What's it to you," Mac said. "This is your last practice."

"What?" Coach Regan said.

A stunned silence filled the room.

"What did you say?" Coach Regan asked again.

"They're meeting right now to see who's going to get the number one job, and it's not going to be you."

"For your information, I never wanted to be head coach. When the league dismissed Coach Murphy, I requested that another coach be found. But you have no right to say what you just said."

Mac just shrugged.

"Why don't you just sit out this practice, Mac," Coach Regan said.

"Sure thing, boss. By next practice, though, if you're still the assistant, you'll be doing what my father tells you."

"Ignore him, Coach," Lizzy said.

"Yeah," Lee said.

"Let's get out on the ice, boys, uh, and girl," Coach Regan said.

I was angry at Mac, but excited by the support I felt from the rest of the kids. I worked to get my thoughts back onto the game. It was time for practice. Trying to regain my focus, I stood up and followed my teammates onto the ice.

Chapter 26

As we got off the ice, I saw my mother sitting alone at the end of a long bench in the warm room. Wrapped in her old gray coat, she was reading, and did not look up. There was no sign of any of the other kids' parents My stomach churned. Would my father be asked to coach? Or would the next coach be Mr. Mackay? If they asked my father, what would he say? If Papa did coach us, and we got worse, everyone would think even less of him than they already did, and that wasn't much. I didn't want to think about it any more, but I did want to know, one way or another.

"Stas, stop the dilly-dally. Let's go," my mother said.

Hadn't she noticed that she was the only Shark parent around?

"Uh, okay."

I followed her toward the main door. Just as we were leaving, I put down my hockey bag, tied my shoes very slowly, and looked back toward the rink. There was a meeting room off to the side of the rink, just before the Zamboni room.

"Stas, let's go!" Mama said with some irritation.

I picked up my bag and gave the meeting room door one last glance. No sign of any Shark parents. I turned and followed my mother out of the rink. It was quiet outside. The only sounds were from a few idling cars and from my feet shuffling through the sand and broken glass which littered the rough cement of the parking lot. Approaching our car, I wondered why there weren't more flat tires at the rink.

As we drove out of the lot, I said, "So, Mama, what did you do during practice?"

She glanced at me and gave me a funny look, like she was suspicious or curious. I guess that I had never asked that before, and it must have seemed strange.

"Why do you ask?" she asked.

"Uh,..., uh, no reason."

"Stas, you are a terrible fibber. You always have been."

I raised my eyebrows and jerked my head backwards like I was insulted. I didn't want to be terrible at anything!

"That is not a bad thing," she said to me, keeping her eyes on the road as she drove. "It is good. It means that you are an honest person. And so, you do not have to say more."

I hadn't planned to tell her anything about Papa and the coaching. If Papa wasn't asked, I didn't want to hurt their feelings. But now, the way my mother was talking to me, well, it made me want to tell her. I needed to tell someone.

"Uh, Mama, something happened at practice."

"Ay-yi-yi, and I didn't see it, because I was too busy reading a book during your practice. I know I should care more and watch, but–"

"Mama, I don't care whether you watch my practice, and besides, it didn't happen *during* practice!"

"Stas," she said calmly, glancing at me quickly and then returning her eyes to the road, "tell your mama what happened. I can see you are troubled."

I breathed in deeply, and said, "The other parents were meeting during practice to see if they wanted to ask Papa to coach our team."

She raised her eyebrows, blinked, and spoke.

"It's about time someone have a brain in that Shark group. Your papa knows more about hockey than all coaches in the league put together. And, God in heaven, could he play!"

With the car stopped at a red light, she shut her eyes and a dreamy smile came to her face. For a second, she looked like a schoolgirl in love. And then her eyes suddenly opened, and she asked, "But how do they know he knows hockey? Did you tell them?"

"No!" I responded quickly.

But now I would have to tell her that I told Ben, and that Ben told his father, and that his father told all the other grownups. And I would be in big trouble. My father did not want anyone to know about his hockey.

"It's all right. I believe you, and I would not be upset if you did tell. Your father, he is foolish not telling others. People should know. He knows the game and can help young people, but his foolish pride is the problem. He is so afraid of sounding stupid because his English is not good. Who ever heard of quitting English class because you don't know English! No one else knows English, too! That's why they go, but, your father, second day of class, he say, 'I swim in the pooh' instead of 'I swim in the pool.'"

I laughed.

"I never heard that!" I giggled.

"Teacher laughed, too, and your father, he do not like to be laughed at, big hockey star. And that is the end of his English class. He will never learn to be an American."

"Mama, he is learning," I said. Again, I was nervous. Was I betraying my father?

"Huh?"

"Uh, didn't you notice that he doesn't speak Russian in the house any more, or hardly ever?"

My mother pursed her lips and was quiet. That meant that she was thinking.

"You are right. How did I not notice?"

"I think it happened gradually. I didn't notice it either, until I found out he was learning English."

"He started up the class again?"

"No, Mama. He's taking an ESL course on the computer."

"ESL?"

"English as a Second Language."

"How do you learn English on a computer?"

"It's a course you can take online, you know, on the internet. I checked it out. They say words, you repeat. Then they say in Russian and you write in English, and the other way around. There are lots of cartoons where they talk in English, but it's pretty obvious what they are saying in English even if you do not know English."

"Interesting," my mother murmured. "How is it that you know all this?"

"The History button on the computer."

Mama wrinkled her forehead in puzzlement. "What is that?"

"Uh, let's see. Let's say you go to a web site. And then someone sits at the computer next. Well, they can click on the History button to see all the sites that you visited."

My mother still looked confused. I don't think that she even knew what a web site was.

"The History button is like a spy who follows you around all day and writes down everywhere you go and everyone you talk to. Clicking on that button is like looking at his report."

"Ah, that I understand!" Mama said. "There were many spies when Russia was a Communist country. I don't think I like this, what you call it..., this History button."

"It's not so bad. It's pretty useful when you want to go back to a site you like. I'll show you sometime at home. Anyway, do you think Papa will say yes if they ask him?"

"Do you think they will ask him?" my mother responded.

"I think so. Mac's father is the only parent interested, but I don't think people like him too much, except Mac. And Coach Regan doesn't want to be head coach. I think they'll ask Papa."

"Aah," she said.

"So, will he do it?" I asked.

"I don't know. There's a lot I don't understand about your Papa. He is a good man, though. What he does, he does very well. It is his pride. It is his great strength and great fault."

"If he doesn't coach us, Mac's father will!"

"Then, you want your Papa to coach your Sharks?"

For the first time, I was sure that I did want that.

"Yes," I said.

"You tell him," my mother said.

"That works for Katya, but not me."

"Because you never try. You are always afraid he will say no, and you do not want to lose, so you pretend that you do not care yes or no. In some ways, you are like your father."

I didn't know if that was a compliment or an insult, but I kind of liked it.

I had been so engrossed in my talk with my mother that I did not realize that we were off the highway. In fact, we were turning the corner to our street! I wondered what the decision had been. Or was the meeting still going on? Maybe it got nasty. Had my father received a call?

Chapter 27

I hopped out of the car and raced across the lawn and up the front stairs.

"Your hockey bag!" my mother called out from the street.

Ignoring her, I opened the front door, ran up to our apartment, and whipped open our apartment door. My father was standing in the doorway, arms folded, wearing a stony expression. That was not good.

"Uh, hi Papa," I said meekly.

He said nothing.

Clang, bang, clunk, bump. I heard my hockey bag being dragged up the apartment stairs, one step at a time.

"What kind of boy makes his mother carry up his hockey bag?" my father said.

A very nervous one, I thought, but I said nothing.

"Ah, Nikolay," my mother said, huffing and puffing as she reached the apartment landing.

My father said nothing. He just glared at us. My mother forced a nervous smile to her face.

"Uh, Papa, did anyone call?" I asked.

My eyes traveled to Yuriy, who was standing near the kitchen, almost hiding behind the door. Yuriy nodded yes.

"If we are going to talk, let us talk inside," my mother said, and practically bowled me over pulling my hockey bag through the doorway.

"Let us sit down and talk like an American family," my mother said.

My father stepped aside to let her in.

"Stas, Nikolay, please sit!"

I stepped to the couch and sat down. My father shuffled to his chair and plopped into it.

"So," I said, breathing in deeply, "did someone call and ask you to coach the Sharks?"

"Yes," he said. "Mr. Leland, he call me. Who is this Mr. Leland?"

"Mr. McSweeny," I said. "Leland McSweeny. He owns the Shark franchise."

"How does one own a youth hockey team?"

"I don't know," I said, "but he does. He must have asked you because all the parents want you to be their coach."

"Why?"

"Because you played on the Red Army team."

"How do they know about my hockey in Russia?" he asked with an edge in his voice.

"It's my fault," I said. "I'm sorry. I know you didn't want me to say anything. I am sorry."

"You told whole team?"

"I told one boy," I said. "I told Ben. And then Ben told his father and Ben's father did not want Mr. Mac to be the head coach, so he told the others."

My father nodded, showing no emotion.

"I'm sorry I disobeyed," I said, "but I'm not sorry that they know if it means that you'll be our hockey coach. We need a good coach, really bad. What did you say?"

I held my breath, waiting for an answer.

"I said I would think about it," he said.

"Papa, please be our coach!"

"Yeah, Papa," Katya called out from our bedroom. I didn't even know that she had been listening. "And if you coach, I can sometimes skate in your practices, like Mr. O'Neil's little kid does at our practices!"

"Katya, hush!" my mother said.

"Papa, we really need you," I said.

"You play like a *galavarez*. I will not allow that. You no backcheck. I make you backcheck. You no get along with teammates. I make you be friends with team. You want that?"

"Oh, yes, Papa!"

"You agree to that, I agree to coach Sharks."

"Thank you, Papa!" I cried.

"Wait until after practice. You might not be so quick to thank me then."

"Oh, I will!"

My mother smiled.

I badly wanted to call Ben and tell him that my father was going to coach the team, but I knew that Papa should call whoever he was supposed to call first. Instead, I walked straight to my room. Yuriy was waiting for me there.

"I can't believe that Papa is going to coach your team!" he said.

"Yeah, I can't either," I said. "Do you think he'll be good?"

Katya walked into the room just at that second, and said, "Of course he'll be great! He was the best player in Russia!"

"Not the best, I don't think," Yuriy said, "but really good. Stas, your other coaches don't know anything. I wonder how good you guys will get?"

"They'll be the best," Katya said. "Just like your team, Yuriy."

"We can't be the best," I said. "We could win all our games and still not be .500 now. We're mathematically out of it."

"You can't be," Yuriy said. "There's still a lot of games left, and I thought that even the tenth place team makes the playoffs."

"The second division playoffs," I said.

"That's better than nothing. Just to make that, for an E Mass team, is pretty good. All the teams in your league are awesome."

"Yeah," I said, "maybe we could make that. But I'll just be happy not to stink anymore. We're the joke of the league."

"So," Yuriy asked, "what did Papa mean when he said that you needed to be friends with the other kids?"

"I don't know. I can't stand Mac. I wonder if that's it. There are groups on the team, like Mac, and Billy. Will is kind of part of those guys. And then there's Ben, me and Lee. Lee is not really one of us now, but he used to be. Then, there are the other guys who are in the middle. Eddie is the only guy that everyone likes. Eddie makes fun of everyone the same, especially himself."

"Yeah, that's not so good. So you're not even friends with Younyoung Lee anymore. What happened with you guys?"

I shrugged my shoulders, but I knew what it was. I knew that it was his parents. They thought I played like a goon, and they did not want that to rub off on their son. And they were right. I had played like a goon. But I really wasn't like that off the ice.

Yeah, Papa was right. We were not a team, and that would need to change for us to get better. But what could he do to change that? How could I help? I would have a hard time being friendly with Mac, but if he got me mad, I could try to at least keep my mouth shut. Maybe I could make things better with Lee. I missed him. School was pretty lonely without him.

I knew that Lee still wanted to be my friend. It was his parents that I had to work on. Before, I'd had an idea, but I never did anything about it. I wasn't about to say I was wrong. I was feeling differently now. I sat down at my desk, took out a piece of paper and a pen, and began to write.

Dear Mr. and Mrs. Lee,

I know that you think that I am not a very nice person, and you are partly right. On the ice, I do get mad, and get too rough with the other team. Part of it is the coach's fault. He tells me to do it. But I made some cheap hits, and that's my fault. I do not want to hurt anyone.

My father is now coaching our Sharks, and things will be different. Younyoung is a very good friend of mine. I hope that you will give me another chance at being his friend.

Sincerely,

Stas

I read over my letter. I had never written anything like this before. I felt like Margaret Cunningham, a girl in school who was always brown-nosing the teacher. It was hard to say I was wrong, and even tougher to write it. But it was even harder to lose a friend.

I put the letter in an envelope, sealed it, and wrote out Younyoung Lee's address. I got up and headed to the kitchen to ask my mother for a stamp.

Chapter 28

"Your old man is a loser," Mac said, whipping his catching glove against the cinderblock wall. The blocker came off next and followed the glove.

"He *is* a butt buster," Eddie said, "and I love it!"

"And I thought my old man was tough," Little Murph said. "Stas, your father is nuts!"

Mac unfastened the two snaps and yanked off his custom painted goalie helmet. He whipped it hard across the black rubber matted floor, banging into Moose's hands as he was unlacing his skates.

"Ow!" Moose said.

"Cut it out, Mac," Woody said.

"Are you stupid?" Little Murph said. "Those goalie masks cost a fortune, don't they?"

"They sure do," Tyler said. "Mine cost two-hundred dollars, and Mac's must have cost a lot more."

"Mac," Sully said. "He worked us all hard. Chill."

"Yeah, but you're playing on Saturday. That stupid Russian lunatic told me I'd be on the bench."

I wasn't mad at Mac for calling my father a stupid Russian lunatic. I had thought that same thing about Papa many times. But Mac, on the bench? Part of me loved it. Mac thought that he was so good that he could be a jerk and not try very hard at practice. But Mac was a lot better goalie than Tyler, and I wanted to win this Saturday. We were playing the Essex Warriors. They were in fifth place. Only a stand-on-his-head-performance by Mac would give us a chance.

"You're not playing?" Billy asked, open-mouthed.

"No," Mac said, pitching a leg pad to the floor. "Good luck, guys."

"We have Tyler in the goal," Ben said. "He'll do fine."

"Yeah," Lizzy said.

Tyler smiled nervously.

Mac laughed. "Against the Warriors? Right!"

"I think we're going to win," Woody said. "This week has been the first time that we have done any defensive work all season. It'll be nice to play with five 'D' instead of two."

My father had spent half of each practice on defensive positioning drills. The forwards worked just as hard as the defensemen on them. Instead of the two wings staying on the boards in the defensive zone, with the center in the middle looking for a breakout pass that never came, the center would back up our defenseman in the corner. Meanwhile the wing covering the weakside point would slide into the upper slot to pick up a second guy out front. Shifting roles as the puck went from one corner to the other was the hardest part. You had to be thinking all the time. But with practice, we got the hang of it. It was like having an extra player in the defensive zone.

"I think that we can win this, too," Moose said. "I like the new defensive scheme. I think Coach Brez knows his stuff."

"Me, too," Drew said.

"The offense will definitely be much better, too," Woody said. "That three-on-three stuff we've been doing, hitting the open man and all, that's going to be big."

"*If* we pass the puck, like Coach says, Will," Billy said, staring right at Will.

"Why are you looking at me?" Will said.

"Duh," Eddie said, "I'm the dumbest kid on the team, and even I know that."

"You need to pass the puck more," Woody said.

"I pass!"

"Yeah," Sully said, "you pass when there's no more room to stick-handle, and you don't have a shot. By then, the other guys have shut off the good passing lanes."

"Will's right," Bake said. "I should know. I've been on your line all season. How many assists do you have?"

"It's not my fault that you guys can't score when I give you the puck!"

"Hey, Will, chill," Sully said. "You're an awesome player. We're just saying you'll be a better one if you pass more. That's what those drills were for."

Will nodded.

"And if you don't pass, be prepared to sit," Mac said. "I'll keep a spot on the bench nice and warm for you."

"Hey, Mac, stuff it," Billy said.

"What, did they even get to you?" Mac asked Billy. "I thought that you were my friend!"

"Did *who* get to me?"

"The Commies!"

"Stop the Commie garbage," Billy said. "It's getting old. Listen, I was just as mad as anyone when Joey and Earl got cut from the team, but you know what? They weren't as good as Ben, Stas and Little Murph, and even Lizzy. I don't know about you, Mac, but I want to win. Coach Brez seems to know hockey. I'm pumped to play the Warriors."

"With Tyler in the goal?"

"Mac, did anyone ever tell you you're a loser?" Sully said. "Tyler's fine. Maybe if you work as hard as he does in practice, you'll get a chance to play."

"Right! The Zamboni driver hates me because little Ruskie there cries to his daddy about mean old Mac. I'll never see any game time this season."

"Give him a try," Lee said. I was shocked! Younyoung Lee actually said a word in the locker room! He continued in his soft voice, "These have been the best two practices of my life. Coach Brez is fair. Give him a chance."

Mac just shook his head.

I was feeling pretty good as I unwrapped the tape from my hockey socks. After ripping off both long strands of tape, I tossed them over to Tyler. Tyler smiled, as he added it to his team tape ball, a mixture of black, white and turquoise, which was now as big as a basketball. Luckily, Tyler's huge goalie bag could still fit the ball in.

"Hey, Tyler," Eddie said, "what are you going to do when the ball gets too big for your bag?"

"He'll stick it up your butt," Will said, grinning. "It's big enough."

"It sure is!" Eddie said, grinning back and slapping his chunky rear end through his bulky hockey pants. "I built it up with Boyd. And there's a lot of poisonous gas stored up in there!"

"Save it for the Warriors," Moose said.

The Warriors. I couldn't wait for the game.

Chapter 29

I was as excited as I had been for the first game of the season. That was back when we thought that we were good, when we thought we could beat anyone. That was back when I was dreaming of the Montreal Cup. Recently, though, we had gone into each game sure that we would lose. There's nothing worse in a sport. It makes you almost not want to play.

Not only were we about to play the strong Essex Warriors in our home rink, but after the game, Ben and I were going over to Lee's house to spend the night! Lee had called us both the night before to ask us. His parents must have gotten my letter, but Lee did not mention that. I wondered if they had even told him about the letter I wrote. I didn't care, though. I was just so excited about going over there, hopefully to celebrate our victory, and to just be friends again.

All the kids on the team wanted my father to make the ice before our game, and so we met as a team even earlier than normal. My father did not say much. He told us to remember what we practiced, work hard, and to have fun. Then he and Coach Regan left. It was just us, alone as a team, for the fifteen minutes before we went on the ice. It was strange. We were used to being lectured forever before games. At first, we just looked at each other. Then Sully started to talk about the team and playing hard and passing. He sounded almost like a coach. Woody said a few things to get us psyched, too. And then other kids started talking as well. Even Will told the kids that we had to pass the puck! Mac sat sullenly at the end of the bench, and was about the only one not to say a word.

By the time the horn sounded, we were totally psyched to play. Coach Regan stuck his head in our team room, and said, "Let's go, boys!"

"Go Sharks!" we all screamed.

I was bursting with energy as my skates hit the ice. I prayed that the Warriors would not score a couple of quick ones. We were riding high, but our bubble could burst very quickly. And if that happened, I did not want to see the smirk that Mac would certainly lord over us.

We skated, stretched, and lined up to shoot on our goalie. Tyler stepped into the net first. That was something new. As we peppered him with shots, he seemed to play with a little something extra. Maybe he was in a zone. I hoped so.

Mac stepped in, and listlessly steered a few shots aside. One or two went by. Tyler took the final shots, and then we returned to the bench.

"Boys," my father said in his thick Russian accent, "short shifts. Leave nothing on ice. One hundred percent." He pronounced 'percent' *pissend.* "In Russia, we say, 'skate *da pateri poolsa,*' so hard, you have no pulse."

"Yeah!" a lot of the guys said.

"Play with pride," my father said. "Play smart. No stupid penalty. Go!"

Sully led the team again, as we all said, "Gooooooo, Sharks!"

My line was on the ice first, with Eddie and Woody on defense. My father had switched the defensive pairs, so our two big guys, Eddie and Moose, were on with different partners. Coach Murphy had liked both the big guys on the ice together for the first shift to set the tone and punish the opponent. My father believed in balancing the pairs.

As we lined up for the opposing face-off, I heard a couple of the guys on the other team snickering about the Zamboni guy. Did they recognize him? Or had they read about him on the E-

Board? There was lots of talk all week about "Zamboni Brez" taking over the Sharks. At first, people thought it was a joke, but once they printed some statistics from my father's years with the Red Army team, the tone changed.

The moment the puck was dropped, we were a different team. We didn't blow away the Warriors. The Warriors were too good. But we played with them. The action went up and down the ice, with neither team getting any great scoring bids. We changed on the fly, and I was exhausted. I had skated *da pateri poolsa*. I hadn't left anything on the ice. I had spent it all. I so wanted to win. Sully's line did the same, and so did Lee's line. Tyler didn't have to make any great saves, but he made a number of solid ones, and controlled all the rebounds. At the end of the first period, there was no score.

In our thirty seconds between periods, all my father said was, "Good job. Keep up."

The second period was much like the first. We had our first power play early on, and set up some great shots, but their goalie made two incredible saves. We didn't score. Near the end of the period, we had our first man in the box. Eddie got called for roughing, but it was a clean hit. The kid he hit was tiny and went down hard, and so they called Eddie.

We worked the box well on defense, and Tyler had one amazing glove save. I don't even think he saw it. It was a point blank shot, and Tyler flipped his glove up, and the puck went in. It was a look-what-I-found save, but he stopped it, and that was what counted. Going into the third period, the score was still tied 0-0.

The Warriors jumped out for the lead in the first shift of the third period. It was on a slap shot from the point where one of their forwards completely screened Tyler. Drew should have pushed the guy out from in front, and he felt bad about that. The lead didn't last long, though. Will actually passed the puck on a 3-on-2, and set up Lee for a top shelf goal. The score remained knotted at one for most of the period.

Warrior frustration grew. They had expected this to be an easy game. We had two power plays from a boarding and roughing call, but couldn't score. With a minute to go, their center hit Tyler after the whistle. Eddie flew in there and was about to flatten him, but instead of cross-checking him, like he usually did, Eddie just bumped him away from our goalie. For once, their guy went out, and Eddie remained on the ice.

My line was put out for our final power play, with Eddie and Moose playing at the points. We controlled the puck and took it up ice, and quickly set up in the offensive zone. We cycled the puck, trying to set someone up in front, but their defense was solid. I passed the puck back to Eddie, who faked a big slap shot, and wheeled around the charging opponent. Eddie slid the puck to Ben on the left. I broke to the far post, where Ben hit me with a perfect pass and I slammed it in the open side of the net. Goal!

My teammates smothered me! It was as if we had won the Stanley Cup! After I pushed my way out from underneath the pig pile, I looked at the scoreboard: Home 2 Visitor 1. Twenty three seconds remained in the game. Their guy came out of the box, and Sully's line went out for us. The Warriors got one shot on goal, a long wrist shot from outside the blue line, which Tyler easily saved. The seconds ticked away and the horn sounded. We had won! We had beaten the Essex Warriors! This time, it was Tyler that got smothered. He had played a great game in the nets. And we had beaten a first division team!

We lined up for the post-game handshake, floating on air. Seeing the shocked and angry faces of the Warriors was sweet. They were good sports, though. I was at the end of the line, just ahead of my father and Coach Regan. I heard the Warrior coach say to Papa, "Nice game, Nikolay. Welcome to the league."

When we got to our team room, we sat down as we always did for Coach Murphy's half hour talks. My father entered the room a moment later, along with Coach Regan. The kids immediately quieted down and looked to my father.

"You did good," he said, without a trace of a facial expression.

Silence followed. Didn't my father know that the coach is supposed to talk more about the game? Even if he has not coached before, he should know about these kinds of things. He had played a ton of hockey in his life.

My father looked toward Coach Regan, who shook his head, meaning he had nothing to add. More silence followed. I was mortified. It looked like my father had no idea what he was doing! That was all I needed. Mac would never let it go. Please sound like a coach, Papa, I silently begged.

My father nodded to us, and left the room. No one said a word. I prayed someone would break the awkward silence. Did the guys think that my father was stupid? Just a stupid janitor, as Mac said?

Finally Eddie stood up. "That was the best freaking coach talk I ever heard!" he boomed.

"Yeah," Sully said. "Doesn't waste our time trying to sound smart."

"He coaches smart, though," Woody said.

"Yeah," Bake said.

Tears almost came to my eyes. I don't think that I was ever so proud in my life.

"You guys played awesome defense!" Tyler said.

"For once, we knew what our jobs were, and we did them. And you made some nice stops," Moose said back to Tyler.

"Yeah, Tyler!" a few of the kids cheered.

Tyler beamed. I glanced at Mac, who was a lot bigger guy than Tyler. Mac seemed to shrink further into his corner of the bench.

"Let's PARTY!" Eddie screamed, turning on his boom box.

"*Who let the dogs out...*" boomed out from the speakers, almost distorted from too much volume and too much bass.

"Who?" Eddie screamed, along with the music, "Who let the SHARKS out! Who..."

The whole team, or almost the whole team, sang along, screaming 'sharks' over the word 'dogs.' Only Mac was quiet. I sang along, looking at my teammates riding so high, and wondered how many five-and-twenty teams have ever been so happy.

Chapter 30

Ben and Lee huddled behind me, as I clicked on 'Favorites' and then clicked on the E-Board link. I knew that Ben was feeling antsy, waiting for my slow dial-up connection to be made. He had high speed cable internet, which took no time, but I knew our connection would eventually get there. Since my father had taken over the team five weeks earlier, reading the E-Board had become fun again. I couldn't wait to see the latest!

Lots of changes had occurred along with our winning ways. The rumors of all the kids leaving the Sharks had ended. In fact, we had just the opposite problem now. The phone in our house was ringing every night with parents trying to get their kids on the Sharks for the next season! My father refused to even talk to new families about that until our season was over. Meanwhile, Papa told the kids on our team that he hoped they would all stay with the Sharks. They were all invited to return. In E Mass hockey, that is almost unheard of. Coaches are supposed to weed out the weaker kids and replace them with better ones. That's how a team improves. But my father wanted no part of that "dirty game," as he called it. Judging by the way our team was playing, Papa knew what he was doing.

Finally, the Eastern Massachusetts Select Hockey League Electronic Bulletin Board appeared on the computer screen. The E-Board. I wondered whether the E stood for Eastern or Electronic.

I knew Crystal Ball's predictions by heart, but Lee had not seen them. The Lees didn't have internet at their house. Plus, there were probably more last minute comments, which were fun to read. Maybe I would write something, too. I had written a few comments myself in the last month.

I searched for Crystal Ball's message, and found it. I instantly clicked there, and text slowly unscrolled on my computer screen.

SSS 5   FW 3

I still could not believe my eyes. The Framingham Wings were in first place and the runner-ups in the Montreal Cup! I read on.

> No, the Crystal Ball is not cracked. Yes, you are reading right. I think that Saturday nite at Hingham will belong to the Sharks. They are the hottest team in the league. They have won 9 of their last 10. The Sharks need a tie to slip into 10th place and make their div 2 playoffs. The Wings have 1st place clinched. They are looking ahead to their first round of playoffs against the Huskies or Eagles. Against a hot and hungry SSS team, the Wings won't fly. Hungry Sharks need to be fed. Wings are on the menu, hold the barbecue sauce. (Crystal Ball)

I loved it. I looked at Lee, whose face lit up, and then he began to laugh. Ben was cracking up, too. Just then, Yuriy came up behind us.

"Stas," he said, "don't you have that memorized yet?"

I turned around and smiled at him.

"Yes," I said, looking away from the computer. "Wings are on the menu, hold the barbecue sauce."

Yuriy smiled back at me.

"Hey, Yuriy," Lee asked, "how did you do last night? Those were your finals, right?"

"Yeah," Yuriy sighed, "we lost. And to the third place team! We beat them twice in the season. Their goalie stood on his head the whole game. We couldn't *buy* a goal."

"You still ended out in first place, though, right?" Lee said.

"Yeah," Yuriy answered. "It was a good season."

"We ended out in second place in our league," Katya said, "and we would have won everything if they had playoffs. Playoffs don't start until Squirts."

"How many goals did you get?" Lee asked.

"I got six goals," Katya stated proudly.

"She's the man," Ben said.

"No," Katya said, "I'm the *woman*." She stood defiantly, hands on hips, eyes dancing with laughter. She was a little cute, even if she was my sister and drove me nuts most of the time.

"She's going to be something in a couple of years," Ben said.

I didn't know whether he meant, like, as a babe, or as a hockey player.

"Yeah," I said, agreeing with either.

"Where's Coach?" Lee asked, glancing towards the easy chair to his left.

Ben and Lee thought that my father lived in his chair, which sat empty across the room.

"He's out," I said. I actually knew where he was, but didn't say. He was at ESL, English as a Second Language class. He was doing the real class now, not the computer one. The real class was two nights a week in Quincy. He had missed one for a practice on Wednesday, and was going to the Saturday afternoon makeup class. He didn't want anyone to know he was going, but at least he went. It made my mother very happy. He'd be home after we ate dinner.

"Let's read the comments!" Ben said.

Most of them were in purple, which meant that I had read them already, but there were a few new ones. There were about twenty-five responses to Crystal Ball's prediction. Most said he was nuts. I clicked on the latest messages.

> Join the 21st century. Crystal Balls are a thing of the past. Time for computerized predictions. No way can the Sharks skate with the Wings. (PWMJ dad)

PWMJ stood for Pee Wee Major, our level. I read more comments below.

> Hah hah hah. Crystal Ball has switched profeshuns. As a comedien, he has promise. (anon)

I smiled at the terrible spelling. It was pretty typical in chat rooms and on electronic bulletin boards, especially the E-Board. I wasn't sure whether people did that on purpose, or if they were just hurrying too much. Or maybe they just couldn't spell. I read on.

> Everytime they say SSS can't do something, Zamboni B comes thru. SSS have much more talent than anyone thought. Took a coach to turn that into success. Zamboni B has never lost on his home ice. Don't count out the South Shore boys yet. (PWMJ observer)

I figured that one was a Shark father.

> True. Home ice means more to Zamboni B than other coaches. How many other coaches make their own ice? Now, that's a home ice

advantage. Haven't heard from you guys who laughed at Z-man at first. Where have you gone? At least admit you were wrong! (dad of 3)

Never count out a team with a hot goalie, and both Shark net minders have been on fire, especially the Truck. They are both better than Ross from the Wings. I like the Sharks.

That message wouldn't last long. It had a player's name in it. It's funny. The writer knew enough to use Mac's nickname, 'the Truck,' as in a Mac truck. But Ross was mentioned by name. The E-Board censor would delete it soon. I wondered who wrote it? Was it a Shark parent? Maybe it was Mac's father, but I expect that there would have been more misspelled words from him. Plus, Mac's father would never say anything good about Tyler.

I had to admit, though, Mac had been playing the best he ever had. For a while, I wasn't sure he'd play at all. After my father took over, Mac just gave half an effort at practice, waiting for Tyler to fall apart and have my father put him back in. But it didn't happen. And even if Tyler had started to play poorly, my father never would have played Mac unless he tried. My father had benched Will against the Huskies, because he wouldn't pass the puck. Papa played Peter, our alternate, instead, and Peter was not half as good as Will. Finally, I guess, Mac just decided that winning was fun and he wanted to be part of it. Or maybe he figured that he could actually learn something from my father. Whatever the reason, Mac just showed up one day to practice, and he wasn't Mac anymore. He worked as hard as anyone, and the next game, he played a period. Since then, Mac and Tyler had split the job of goaltending.

My eyes returned to the E-Board.

> Crystal Ball, your totally rong! (PWMJ def)

> Crystal Ball, you are cracked!   (FW parent)

> I never will change my predictions, or hedge
> my bets, but I have never seen my prediction
> cause so many strong feelings. If FWs have
> been reading, they now have a reason to win.
> Sorry for giving them one, Sharks. I still like
> SSS, but count on a battle to the end. (Crystal
> Ball)

Suddenly I was nervous. I had counted on jumping on an
over-relaxed Wing team, and taking the game away before they
even knew what had happened. I expect that Crystal Ball was
right. After all that had been written, the Wings would be
pumped. But reading is one thing, and seeing is another. They
had killed us twice. Deep down, they still had to expect an easy
game, and it would not be easy. The team they would be playing
against that night would be nothing like the Shark team they
had mauled twice.

"We'll beat them," Lee said calmly. "We will win because our
players are just as good, and our coach is better."

"You guys will definitely win!" Katya said.

I heard the doorbell ring.

"Is it Coach?" Ben asked.

"No," I said. "He doesn't ring the bell. He lives here!"

"Who is it, then?" Yuriy asked.

"I think it's one of my friends," Katya said, and she ran to
answer the bell.

"Lizzy!" Katya said, as she opened the door.

"Hi, Katya," Lizzy said, stepping inside, dragging her hockey bag.

Ben and Lee turned to me, both giving me a questioning look.

"What's Lizzy doing here?" Ben whispered.

"I don't know," I said, but I was kind of glad it was Lizzy.

"Hi, guys," Lizzy said. "I hope you don't mind that I came over. Katya invited me."

"Oh, no, I'm glad you're here," I said, then worried that I sounded a little too glad. That would not be cool. But she was on my team, and she was a good kid, and she and Katya had become buddies. Lizzy was almost an assistant coach on Katya's hockey team. Plus, Lizzy had invited Katya and me to play shinny hockey at Meadows Prep a couple of times. It was just us and Lizzy's whole family playing full ice games. So it was like Lizzy and I were friends, hockey friends.

A delicious smell wafted in from the kitchen. I had forgotten what my mother was cooking for our early dinner.

"Mmm!" Ben said. "What's that I smell?"

"Wait till you see," Yuriy said, and smiled.

"Yeah!" Katya said, and giggled.

A moment later, my mother came into the living room, and said, "Come to the kitchen, and eat!"

We all followed our noses to the kitchen, where a platter sat in the middle of the table, stacked high with barbecued chicken wings.

"Wings!" Ben said as soon as we were seated. "I love these things! We have them every year on Super Bowl Sunday."

"I love wings, too," Lee said.

"Don't you guys get it?" Yuriy asked.

"What?" Ben asked.

"I get it," Lizzy said, smiling.

"Tell me!" Ben said.

"Wings!" Yuriy said. "We're feasting on wings for dinner!! Wings, you know, like the Framingham Wings."

"Oh, yeah!" Ben said. "Cool! But you didn't hold the barbecue sauce!"

Everyone laughed.

"Where's Papa?" Katya asked. "Isn't he eating with us?"

"He'll be home in an hour," my mother said.

"So, why don't we wait for him?" Katya asked. "The game isn't until much later."

"He told us that the boys should not eat just before leaving for the game. So we eat early. Come! Eat up!"

Within minutes, our mouths and hands were all a red, sticky mess. Wings for dinner, I thought, and Wings tonight for dessert, Framingham Wings.

Chapter 31

I almost threw up. I was sucking for more air as I stepped onto the bench. Our only chance against these Wings was to skate each shift as if it were the only one we would play in the game. I was doing that as I never had before. I was skating *da pateri poolsa*. So were all the Sharks. And with thirty seconds left to play in the second period, we were in the game. The score was tied, 2-2.

Mac had been playing the best I had ever seen him play. The Wings had not come out flat, as Crystal Ball predicted. They were gunning for us as if they had something to prove. Thanks, Crystal Ball. Well, we were skating and hitting every bit as hard. We knew that we had to tie the game to be guaranteed a playoff spot. If we lost, we had to hope that the Islanders tied or lost the next day. I did not want to have to rely on another team winning for us to make the playoffs, and I was not ready to hang up my skates for the season.

The horn sounded, ending the second period. We just had to hold them off for twelve more minutes, and we would be in the playoffs! And then I remembered that Tyler was supposed to play the third period. They alternated who played one and who played two periods. Usually we had a couple goal lead by the third period, so putting in a cold goalie wasn't too risky, but I was worried about this game. The Wings could pass like no other team, and every one of their forwards was a sniper. I knew that putting Tyler in the net would be the right thing, and my father usually did the right thing. Only I was hoping that he wouldn't just then.

"We can hold 'em," Woody said. "One more period. All we need is a tie."

"No!" my father said. "No tie. Tie be to kiss your sister, they say in America. In Russia we say something different, but you are too young to hear that. But this Wing team, it is supposed to be best, no?"

We nodded.

"You Sharks, you are the best. Win."

"What about the playoffs, Coach?" Bake asked. "All we have to do is tie and we make the playoffs."

"Playoffs, shmayoffs," my father said. "I no care. You beat Wings, you are the best. Win it."

The ref's whistle blew. Sully led the team with a booming, "Go Sharks!" The fans were cheering and screaming for us. The building was rocking!

Tyler was sitting behind me, and didn't move. Mac turned around and headed back to our goal. Wasn't Tyler going in?

I turned back to Tyler and said, "I thought that you were playing the third this game?"

"I was supposed to, but Mac was playing so well that Coach asked me if I would mind sitting this one out. He said that he'd play me the full game the next game. It would be tough going in cold against this Wing team, so I was actually kind of relieved that he asked me."

I held out my glove to Tyler, and he tapped it back with his blocker.

"Hey, what are those little white things on your helmet?" They looked like little dots.

"Oh, I paint one of those dots on every time we win a game that I play in. I can't afford to get one of those paint jobs like Mac has, but this makes my mask cool, too."

"Yeah, it does," I said. "And if we win, make sure to add another dot, even if you don't play. Not many goalies would volunteer to sit out. Mac is unbelievable out there tonight."

My line shifted over on the bench. We were about to go out. My father signaled for a line change, and I was on the ice. The signal is for forwards, not for defense, but Eddie began to skate to the bench. I could see their wing was going to get to the loose puck at center ice, and maybe have a breakaway! I sprinted as fast as I could, but it was not fast enough. Their guy had jets and had me by two steps. I dove forward, and swung my stick hard at his skates. The kid went down and the ref blew the whistle.

The Wing fans were screaming.

"Intent to injure!" one yelled. "Kick the Russian kid out!"

The Wing coaches ran out to their injured player. He moved his leg slowly. I breathed a sigh of relief. A minute later, the kid was helped to his feet, and held on to two teammates as he left the ice on one skate.

All the players on both sides tapped sticks on the ice.

"Penalty shot!" another Wing fan yelled.

"Two minutes, tripping," the ref said to the scorekeeper.

"Why isn't it a penalty shot?" Bob Bailey, the Wings coach, screamed. I had read about Coach Bailey a lot on the E-Board.

"Their left defense might have caught him. Not a clean breakaway," the ref answered.

"Gimme a break!" Coach Bailey yelled.

"I'm warning you, sir," the ref said, and the Wings coach turned away.

I skated to the box, praying that Mac would hold them. As I slammed the door to the penalty box shut, I wondered if my father would be mad at me. He had told us before the game that the Wings had the best power play in the league, and we needed to keep it off the ice to win. So far, we had been in the box just once, for a cheap hitting-from-behind call, which was really from the side. The Wings had scored in about twenty seconds.

We had our fastest, strongest guys out there. The Wings quickly controlled the puck, and our box moved well to contain them. For a minute we limited them to outside shots, which Mac easily stopped. Finally, at a whistle, we changed lines. Moose and Drew were on 'D', with Lizzy and Ben our forwards. There were forty-five seconds left to go in the penalty.

The Wings moved the puck in and out of the corners like pros, when suddenly their left point broke toward the net and was hit with a perfect pass from the left corner. Their big defenseman one-timed a perfect slap shot. It went so fast I didn't even see it. I just saw the twine move over Mac's shoulders, and saw him slam his stick to the ice. We were behind, 3-2.

The ref opened the door to let me out of the box. I skated sluggishly back to the bench. Lizzy and Ben tapped me five. My father stepped over to me.

Oh, no, I thought.

"Good penalty," he said.

I looked at him, puzzled.

"You needed to stop breakaway."

"But I hurt him."

"You did not do that on purpose. Hockey is a rough game."

"But we're behind, now!"

"Still lots of time," he said, and moved back to his usual spot next to Coach Regan.

A minute later, Eddie got cross-checked, and they had a guy go off. We had our third power play of the game. We hadn't scored on one yet, but we needed to here. There were just four minutes left to play.

Billy, Murph and Sully were put out on offense. Sully had been our big scorer lately. Eddie and Moose, our defensemen with the best shots, were together on the points. The Wings had really quick forwards on their penalty killing team. Every time we broke the puck out of our zone, they intercepted a pass, and ragged the puck for as long as possible, then dumped it back into our end. I saw my father getting ready to call a line change. The Wings had their two forwards deep in our zone, skating into and out of the corners, and passing the puck to each other. The seconds ticked by. And then Sully flew out of nowhere and intercepted a pass, flying up ice as fast as he could. His left and right wing were with him, breaking into Wing territory on a 3-on-2. All day we had passed to the wing on odd man rushes. Sully faked a pass to Billy, then accelerated to the net. He caught both Wing defensemen leaning the wrong way, splitting their 'D' and going in alone on their goalie.

Please, Sully, I prayed. Their goalie came out of the net hard, a little too hard. Sully faked to his forehand, and shifted the puck to his backhand, and slid it into an open Wing net.

Our bench erupted! The fans screamed! We had tied the game! Against the first place Wings!

My line was out next, with just a minute and a half to play. All we had to do was to hold on for a tie, and we would be in the playoffs!

The Wings controlled the face-off, and dumped it into our zone. And then I noticed that the Wing goalie was sprinting to their bench. What was going on?

The puck was tied up in our corner for a face-off in our zone. And then I realized what was happening. They were lifting their goalie for an extra skater. But it was a tie game! No one pulls a goalie in a tie, unless it's a must-win game, and it wasn't for the Wings. But it was a must-tie game for us. And then I knew what they were doing. They were trying to knock us out of the playoffs.

The Shark fans were booing.

"Cheap! Cheap!" Mac's father yelled.

Pockets of Wing fans were cheering.

What were we supposed to do defensively? We had not practiced a 6-on-5 situation! The puck was dropped. We controlled in the corner, but two Wings knocked the puck away from Woody. They flipped it in front of the net, where one of their two centers fired it at Mac. It deflected off Mac's facemask and went behind the net. Moose picked it up and passed to Lizzy along the left board. Lizzy flipped the puck to center ice, where a Wing defensemen controlled it. Ben checked him hard, and the puck was knocked loose. It was right in my path to the goal. I accelerated as hard as I could and got to the puck just as their other defenseman did. It was on my backhand, but I couldn't muscle it forward. Instead, I flipped the puck toward the empty net. It bounced slowly, right toward the goal. Their other defenseman was flying in to stop the puck. He dove, but just missed. My shot rolled across the goal line. We were ahead!

My team went crazy! They surrounded me and cheered. I said that it was Ben who set it up with his hit. They all high-fived Ben. Finally our line skated to the bench.

"Good goal, boys," Coach Regan said. My father just nodded to me.

"Papa, wasn't that cheap, them pulling their goalie in a tie? They just wanted to knock us out of the playoffs!"

"Not cheap. Wing coach does not want tie. Maybe he's got some Russian in him."

I saw a trace of a smile form at the corner of my father's mouth. I wondered what Papa meant.

The Wings kept their extra skater on the ice, but the wind had gone out of their sails. The Wings could not fly. That's what I'd say when I wrote about this game on the E-Board. In no time, the game was over. Our guys flew off the bench and almost crushed Mac. Luckily. Mac wore goalie equipment or else he might have been really hurt. The mighty Wings stood at center ice in a line, waiting to shake our hands. Half of their guys didn't say a word to us. One swore at each of us. They weren't very good losers. I guess they didn't have much practice at it.

That moment, those final seconds in our win against the Wings, was the highlight of the season. We had beaten the second best Pee Wee team in the world. Maybe we were the best. We went on and easily won the E Mass Division II playoffs. Tyler had a shutout against Big Gun, and Mac and Tyler split the final game against Brockton, which we won, 6-1. The local newspapers did big stories on my father, both as a Shark coach and as a former Red Army team player. No one ever called him *just* a Zamboni guy after that. The Zamboni stuck, though, and everyone called him Zamboni Brez, everyone except his players, who called him 'Coach.'

I'm a second year Bantam now. I go to school with Ben at Meadows Prep, and we play hockey together there and with the Sharks. My father only assists with coaching the Sharks because he is also in charge of Katya's Triple-A Girl's Squirt team from Hanover. Last year, he led them to a state championship. This year, he wants to take them to the nationals in Minnesota. Yuriy is the only one of us not to have Papa for a coach. Next year, though, Yuriy will play for the Sharks, and Papa promised to at least help out with the coaching.

It's hard to believe that my father has been coaching less than three years in this country. It seems like everyone knows him! Whenever we step into a rink together, no one ever says, "Stas, hey Stas!" It's always, "Brez! Zamboni Brez!" It doesn't matter what rink we're at or who's playing. And every time I hear those words, and hear the respect and love in that greeting, I am proud to be my papa's son, the son of Zamboni Brez.

Mark Fidler lives in Waltham, Massachusetts with his wife and three sons. Besides teaching high school math and computer science, he has coached youth hockey and Little League baseball.

Also written by Mark Fidler –

Pond Puckster

Baseball Sleuth

Signed Ball

The Call of Sagarmatha

Coming soon: *Blaze of the Great Cliff*

For more information about these books, turn to the following pages, or visit the author's web page at

www.markfidler.com

All books by Mark Fidler are on sale at most online bookstores. Or ask for them at your local bookstore.

How did you like *Zamboni Brez*?
Tell the author! Email him at author@markfidler.com

Pond Puckster

By Mark Fidler

Ten year-old Jason Quinn lives for hockey and has everything that a young hockey star could ever want - he owns the best equipment that money can buy, and he plays for the league's prestigious select team, the Junior Terriers. Best of all, he is planning to travel on the Canadian Hockey Tour with a team of the best young players in the Northeast.

But just months after the death of his father, Jason's dream season crashes to a halt when his mother tells him that they have no more money. Forced out of their wealthy suburban Boston home, Jason must move in with his uncle, aunt and six rough-and-tumble cousins in northern Maine. The older boys, Billy and George, are just plain scary. Working in the potato fields is awful. And being fifty miles from the nearest indoor rink, Jason can't even play on an organized hockey team! Life is not worth living.

Follow Jason through his winter in Glenville, where the only hockey is played on a pond. Experience the joys, sorrows, excitement and fun of that "most important time" of Jason's life. A young Acadian boy raised far from his roots is about to learn more about family, life and hockey than he had ever dreamed.

Baseball Sleuth

By Mark Fidler

"You buried the body in the yard?"

These words, spoken to a man named Bob, crackle from the baby monitor. Phillip strains to hear more through the static. A murder! No one will believe him unless he finds out who Bob is, and where Bob lives.

Phillip Crafts loves baseball but he is a terrible player. He loves mysteries, but his teammates laugh at him when he sees crimes where they don't exist. Meanwhile, at home, his life is even worse. After twelve years of being an only child, Phillip's newborn sister has taken all of his mother's time, energy, and maybe even her love. And he is sure that he can never earn the respect of his "jock" stepfather. The only good thing in his life is his best friend Jackson, the girl next door.

Armed with few clues, Phillip and Jackson work to unravel the mystery of the buried body. Their investigation builds to an exciting and dangerous climax, just as Phillip's baseball season builds toward its final, dramatic game.

Signed Ball

By Mark Fidler

More than anything, eight-year-old Jimmy Jarvis wants a baseball autographed by his favorite major league player, and he is willing to do almost anything to get it. Jimmy has another wish, too. After living in six different foster homes in six years, Jimmy wants a family that will be his forever. But will he risk a chance at a real home for the ball of his dreams?

Follow Jimmy as he plots one wild scheme after another in his quest for that signed ball. And share the moving story of Jimmy's life as a foster child, where he faces choices that no young boy should have to make. Filled with humor and warmth, *Signed Ball* is a story the whole family will enjoy.

The Call of Sagarmatha

By Mark Fidler

Making diving headers on the soccer field or climbing the toughest walls of rock, Mardi Slote lives life to the fullest. Like her father, she fearlessly "pushes the envelope" in all she does. But when her father announces that he is going to climb the world's tallest mountain, a mountain that has already claimed more than a hundred lives, Mardi is afraid.

The Call of Sagarmatha follows David Slote's battle for survival against the elements on Mount Everest, or Sagarmatha, as the native people of Nepal refer to it. Meanwhile, Mardi must struggle with her anger, which threatens to destroy her zest for life, and tear her family apart.

In a novel which captures the drama of climbing, from the rocky cliffs of New Hampshire to the slopes of Mount Everest, the greatest struggle is in the soul of a twelve year-old girl. It's a battle that can only be won with the help of her family, her best friend Jeannie, her climbing partner Arthur, and her pen pal Ngwang, the young son of a Sherpa mountain guide.

Coming soon!

Blaze of the Great Cliff

By Mark Fidler

Above all else, young Blaze wants to be a man of his Sinagua tribe. He dreams of being a great hunter and warrior. But his people of the Great Cliff are a peaceful farming tribe and believe that learning the skills of war will anger the gods and worsen the drought that already threatens all the peoples of the desert. And then, on his first great journey, Blaze discovers the great Hohokam people and their game of guayball, a brutal and exciting sport played by both boys and men. Drawn to that culture which respects fighters above all others, Blaze must decide where his true spirit lies.

Enjoy the excitement, passion and danger of the final days of America's great cliff dwellings. In a world threatened by drought and war, one boy strives to grow up, and do the right thing for himself and his people.

Expected publication date: Summer, 2003